HERR FAUSTINI TAKES A TRIP

Wolfgang Hermann

HERR FAUSTINI TAKES A TRIP
Translated by Rachel Hildebrandt

1st Edition
POD

KBR
Greenville
2016

Publisher **Noga Sklar**
Translation **Rachel Hildebrandt**
Text edition **KBR**
Cover design **KBR**

Title of the original in German *Herr Faustini Verreist*
Copyright © 2015 *Wolfgang Hermann*
All rights reserved.

ISBN: 978-1-944608-04-0
ISBN: 978-1-944608-05-7 (E-book)
Library of Congress Control Number: 2016930094

KBR Digital Publishers LLC.
www.kbrdigital.com
www.facebook.com/kbrdigital
contact@kbrdigital.com

Greenville - SC
1|864|373.4528

FIC000000 — Fiction/ General

Born in 1961 in Bregenz, Austria, **Wolfgang Hermann** studied philosophy in Vienna, after which he traveled extensively and lived in Berlin, Paris, Aix en Provence, and Tokyo. He has published numerous books of prose and poetry, among the most recent: *Abschied ohne Ende* (novel, 2012), *Schatten auf dem Weg durch den Bernsteinwald* (poetry, 2013), *Die Kunst des unterirdischen Fliegens* (novel, 2015), and *Die letzten Gesänge* (stories, 2015). Wolfgang Hermann's numerous prizes include the Juergen Ponto Prize (1987), the Siemens Literature Prize (2002), the Anton Wildgans Prize (2006), and the Austrian State Advancement Award (2007). *Herr Faustini takes a Trip* is the first of his books to be published in English.

E-mail: post@wolfganghermann.at

-1-

The cat's eyes glinted topaz as he lifted his head and snuffled a sunbeam, his whiskers vibrating as if electrified. Smacking his lips quietly and purring in a crescendo, he nestled his head back into the grass and clamped his tail between his two forepaws. His body rose and fell in time with his breathing, and he kept his eyes shut for long spans of time, allowing their yellow to twinkle forth only briefly in between innumerable breaths before his eyes once again vanished deep within. This rhythm set the feline tempo, a tempo which exerted a calming effect over the entire garden, spreading into the house where Herr Faustini was just filling the cat bowl for breakfast.

How long had the vacuum cleaner been wailing this morning? It was a wailing that served a good purpose, because housecleaning could be easily described as a good purpose. Now the wailing had fallen silent, seemingly refusing to budge from where it had come to a stop. Herr Faustini listened. He focused his attention through the wall, close on the heels of Maria, the cleaning woman, who was operating the vacuum. There it was, the tiny tinkling. Herr Faustini's ears had learned with bat-like sharpness to detect this miniscule sound. The vacuum was now running again, but it was not moving. Herr Faustini could see Maria in his mind, how she was standing motionlessly on the other side of the wall and staring at the pile of shards. Did she feel badly about this? Was this typical for her? Was it normal for Maria that each of her visits was accompanied by a crash? Maria had been cleaning for Herr Faustini for several months. And like clockwork, she broke something in the house every time she came. Once it had been a vase that had survived an eternity in a particular nook, until the day that Maria got too close to it. Another time it was a picture that she tried to dust unconventionally, whereby, in the process of being dusted, the picture fell under the effect of Newton's Law of Gravity. The picture plunged to the floor, its glass shattering upon impact. On yet a different occasion, the victim was a small, plump cherub, which Herr Faustini had received as a Christmas gift from his neighbor, Frau Gigele, and which he had suspended from the ceiling by a long, barely visible cord. The cherub seemed to float about halfway up the wall, borne aloft by its incandescent goldenness and its smile which beamed in all directions. As the cherub smashed against the floor, it was suddenly very still in the house. Maria did not dare move. Herr Faustini could hear the silence, and even before he laid eyes on the cherub fragments on the floor, he knew what had happened.

Maria retreated to a far corner of the house and acted busy. Herr Faustini stood with the pieces of the cherub cupped in his hands and thought about nothing. In this particular moment of silence, he wondered what was keeping him from seeking a different cleaning woman. He studied the fragments in his hands again, and suddenly realized that Maria was trying to teach him how to say goodbye to the things he cared about. Since only by first letting go, as Herr Faustini finally comprehended this morning, only by first letting go was he free to take other paths. Wasn't this the very thing that so often struck him about this lovely, tidy country? Everything was cordoned off by property boundaries, the possessors frequently grimacing menacingly as they crouched over their possessions. Finally this morning, it dawned on Herr Faustini that Maria, the cleaning woman, was fulfilling a higher calling when she shattered a vase, a cherub, a frame, and that none of the associated guilt lay with her. Didn't she always look contrite whenever he caught her with the shards? She would repeatedly stammer out something about not seeing or poor fastenings, or she would scold the thing laying in pieces at her feet, as if it had committed a horrendous atrocity by breaking under her feather duster. No, Herr Faustini decided this morning not to give Maria her walking papers. After all, how could he do that, now that he finally understood her true mission?

The vacuum cleaner was sucking up nothing, undoubtedly to buy Maria time to pull herself together. However remorseful she might feel at this point, she could not look Herr Faustini in the eye yet. Besides that, she had a weakness for vacuum cleaner noise, a racket which prevented Herr Faustini, on the other hand, from pursuing any line of thought. He all too readily perceived vacuum noise as an assault on his privacy, and he understood perfectly well why the cat vanished as soon as the vacuum started up. He, too, fled the house occasionally when Maria maneuvered the vacuum through the rooms (actually it was the vacuum that seemingly called the shots), so he could avoid hearing the shattering of the next fragile object. On the other hand, Herr Faustini was afraid that Maria would inflict even greater damage if he left her unattended. The letting go of treasured objects needed to happen in baby steps, one foot after the other. No one had the right to demand that he part with everything all at once, even if it had to eventually come to that. And Maria was the right person to prepare him for that day. The vacuum was no longer running in the neighboring room. Herr Faustini tried not to prick up his ears, but this was a useless endeavor since they pricked themselves up, straining to hear what was going on in the next room. Nothing. Was Maria collecting the pieces? He might have heard a faint clinking. She did not seem to be moving. What was she doing? This is how Herr Faustini had imagined it would be to have a cleaning woman. Within an amazingly short time span, one became the slave of the cleaning woman, doing everything possible in order to not convey the impression that one was a complacent, exploitive jerk, but rather an uncomplicated, sympathetic person. If he were sitting in his office, as he had in the past, during the times that Maria was cleaning his home, he probably would have spent the entire time wondering if everything was going alright, worrying that she had failed to tighten the faucet in the bathroom, to lock the exterior door, to set out fresh water for the cat. No, being gone was not a solution. He would have mentally shadowed Maria the entire time she was cleaning, visualizing his armchair standing under water, his bedroom flooded, and the cat helplessly locked in the bathroom.

The doorbell. Who could that be? Herr Faustini opened the door. A man with a red face and an even redder nose was standing before him. "We're collecting," he said, rather breathlessly.

Herr Faustini looked around. All that was out here was a leaning bicycle, but it was possible that this bike and its man had been on the go together for such a long time that he now viewed the two of them as separate personalities. "We're collecting signatures," he continued as he pushed his glasses back in place and fixed Herr Faustini with a penetrating glare. "They want to open a noise factory here," the red man said. "A discotheque or whatever they call it. We don't want something like that here. It'll bring commotion and vermin to our town."

Vermin? Herr Faustini had to think about this for a moment. What kind of vermin would be attracted to the town because of noise? "You know, all the wrong kind of people would come because of that wretched place."

"Unfortunately, I don't have any time to spare your vermin," concluded Herr Faustini. "We're grappling with a vacuum cleaner problem here in this house. Besides, shouldn't you reconsider your choice of words? When you've had time to think everything through again, then drop back by. I'm in the process of learning how to let things go, which is why my mind's not free to grapple with terminology like this. I'm sure you understand."

The man with the red face traced a rectangle in the air with his head, looked down at the ground, and swung back up on his bike without a word.

Herr Faustini stepped back into the hall, unhooked his jacket, and slipped out of the house. He did not want to see Maria's advice-seeking face, since he had no advice to give.

-2-

With his head thrown back, Herr Faustini stood in front of the bank, gazing up at the facade that rose above him. The bank was expanding, bursting at every seam. The stomach of the bank seemed bulging and full, stuffed, among other things, with the loan repayments that Herr Faustini had deposited here over the many years. I paid for part of this addition, Herr Faustini thought, thanks to interest rates that had been so high that no one today would believe it. The loan has been paid off, my job is now a thing of the past, my time belongs to me alone, thought Herr Faustini. Why should I be upset at the bank, and if I was, which of the employees should I blame? Perhaps the nice Herr Hämmerle who handled my loan papers? Herr Hämmerle is no longer alive. Working at the bank was too much for his heart. Or should I be mad at the nice Frau Nussbaumer, who always offered me a cup of coffee, even if all I needed to do was sign something? Frau

Nussbaumer made me feel like I was actually somebody, and I'm grateful to her for that. It wasn't her fault that she was forced to raise my interest rate. No, Herr Faustini was not angry at anyone, as he studied the new building serenely.

It was reverently silent in the bank. More than just the architectural finishings testified to nicely stuffed wallets, which were also reflected in the courtesy and thoughtfulness of the bank tellers who strove to serve Herr Faustini. It was not surprising that hardly anyone went to church any more. Everyone who wanted to cultivate a good reputation showed up at the bank. There was something quaint about witnessing the propagation of money. The money grew rampantly in closed chambers, odorless and hygienic. Money was power and concentration. Herr Faustini had no idea what he was looking for in the bank, but he felt suspiciously comfortable here. Yes, everyone in the bank was suspicious. Suspicious that one day they would no longer be able to pay back their ongoing debts. Suspicious that from one day to the next they would find themselves among those who were unable to open a bank account anywhere. But the bank was also suspicious. Behind its cordiality and thoughtfulness lay the desire to make its customers dependent on its services. Wasn't it a lovely feeling to be welcomed sincerely by a nicely dressed young woman offering advice on the newest investment, estate planning, and wealth creation products? Yes, Herr Faustini could not shake the suspicion that behind the bank's glittering surfaces, nets were concealed. These nets bound every person here to their place, exactly where they were supposed to be. After all, there was no way out, thanks to all the bank documents that had already been signed. Certainly, modern financial transactions had their conveniences. Certainly, money meant a high degree of freedom to whoever had access to a little of it. But what kind of freedom had to be bought with so much fear?

"How can I help you?" asked a pleasant female voice.

He did not realize, at first, that the question was being directed at him. He was caught somewhere in the midst of the nets and the fear. The pleasant female voice repeated the question. Herr Faustini looked over into the face of Frau Nussbaumer, who was smiling at him cheerfully. She held out to him her delicate hand, which he happily shook. She even asked how he was doing. "Thank you, well," Herr Faustini replied sheepishly.

For whatever reason, he had not calculated on having any actual personal contact with anyone here. Should he admit to Frau Nussbaumer that he was only in the bank to recover from Maria and the vacuum? Frau Nussbaumer would surely be sympathetic. Here in town, the older residents all went to the bank to check on their documents. They frequented the bank because that is what the other senior citizens did, and they could meet each other here. Besides that, it was nice to listen to your money growing somewhere behind the solemn murmuring. That was the reason why the bank was doing so well that it could expand. It was a little tight in the counter area because of the crowd of people there. One person after the other disappeared into the individual cubicles for consultations, but the flow of people into the bank never abated. On some mornings, it was as if they were handing out presents here.

Herr Faustini pulled out his billfold and removed a hundred-euro bill. "Could you please change this for me?" he asked, ashamed that he could not come up with anything better.

Frau Nussbaumer politely led him to the counter, gave instructions to the young lady there, and bid Herr Faustini goodbye with a handshake. Herr Faustini wanted to say something to Frau Nussbaumer. He felt the empty space behind his forehead, opened his mouth but then hesitated before thanking her courteously. He picked up the smaller bills and quickly left the bank.

Out on the street, it occurred to him that he had not yet experienced the calming effect of a drive today. Across the way, the bus to Bregenz was just about to pull out. He waved at the driver, crossed the street, and boarded. The bus glided gently around the curve. Herr Faustini swayed back and forth with the motion of the vehicle, as the deep blue lake emerged in front of him.

-3-

Can hydrophobia be a visible attribute? Herr Faustini sat by the lake as he usually did. He maintained a little distance from the two young mothers whose small children were digging away in the lakeshore with plastic shovels. Herr Faustini was not unsociable, but he did value his peace and his view of the lake. He picked a spot close to a darkly tanned, older man in skimpy swimming trunks, who was sitting on a towel about twenty paces off. In comparison to this man, Herr Faustini looked quite pale and perhaps a little unathletic. But sunbathing was not really his thing, and he could count on one hand the number of times he went swimming in the lake in a given year. There was nothing Herr Faustini could do to change his appearance.

Suddenly a tanned, middle-aged lady in short trousers and a sleeveless shirt strode to the water's edge to bend down and rinse her hands in the lake. She glanced at Herr Faustini and commented: "You're scared of the water, right?" Herr Faustini must have looked rather puzzled, because she continued: "You're definitely afraid of the water. There's something about you, you know. I can always spot the hydrophobes. You aren't possibly a writer, are you? I used to work in a convalescent home for writers. The lake was right out the front door. Do you think that even one of them ever went in the water? Day after day, they'd stroll around the lake with books stuck under their arms. It was eight kilometers, mind you. Once they'd done that, they'd sit down in the shade and read. For hours, they'd just sit there and read, as quiet as mice. Working with them was pretty dull, each one paler than the next. There's nothing anyone can tell me about writers that I don't already know. They're such bores. And they're always willing to steal book ideas from one another, which is why they don't like each other. And they think so highly of themselves, as if they were the Emperor of China or something. Anyway, they all had one thing in common, their fear of water. Considering that, they should have had plenty to talk about. You don't happen to be a writer?" the woman in trousers asked once again. "Your paleness would be just about right for that, and I've never seen you in the water. I often see of you sitting down here at the lake, gazing off in the distance. Of course, you don't have a book with you, which would speak against you being a writer, but I suppose there might be authors out there who never read any books. Perhaps they're too good to read books written by other people. But when I look closely at you, you don't seem arrogant enough for that. Are you sure that you aren't even just a little bit of a writer?"

Herr Faustini reached for an answer, but the lady had already pulled off her trousers and sleeveless shirt, proudly displaying her well-toned, swimsuited body before diving into the lake. After swimming out a short way, her head resurfaced several meters from shore, and she picked up the line of conversation where she had left off. Her voice grew increasingly softer the further out she swam. Murmuring in a low voice, Herr Faustini asked: "Is it really that easy to be a writer? Is it enough if you gaze at a lake more than you swim in it? I don't personally know the ladies and gentlemen who write, but I do know that they deserve to be respected highly because they strive to depict another world. Not just anyone can be good at that. I wouldn't be able to come up with a single word worth writing down. It wouldn't even occur to me to write anything. Isn't it proper to give everything the time and space it needs? But while someone's writing about this or that, don't the boundaries of space and sometimes time expand? Without writing, the things that aren't written down only exist in one particular moment, and then they're over. That's the way it should be, I think. But somehow we've grown accustomed to the world's wordiness, in both its spoken and written dimensions. Week after week, they come and empty the recycling containers after they've been fattened with words. Wouldn't it be better if there was less of this? The ladies and gentlemen who write face a difficult task of counteracting the wordiness and only writing that which allows some form of the world to express itself. Things shouldn't grow darker because of a book, but brighter and somehow clearer. I don't think that's just a minor point. Whoever can do this is not simply writing for the recycling bin. I could never be someone like that, but I do respect those who write in hopes of unearthing the things long buried under the mountains of words."

Herr Faustini watched the swimmer move further out into the lake. He stood up discreetly and walked toward the city, convinced that he had earned an ice cream.

At home, the shards were still tinkling in the garbage can. Maria had bent over them for a long time, as if there were something she could actually do about them. The cat slipped through the rooms, skirting around the tinkling. That's what Herr Faustini saw in his mind.

-4-

The moment Herr Faustini opened his eyes, he knew it was one of those days. On a day like this, time stood stock still, life refused to budge, and everything congealed into a small, ugly clump. Was Herr Faustini's life really supposed to be like this, like this clump? All because a mass of leaden clouds was pressing down on his house? Herr Faustini could feel the corners of his mouth sink, and even his ears were hanging lower than usual (but hadn't the ears of Gautama, known as the Buddha, grown longer with his advancing enlightenment?). At least, his eyes were open, thanks to the fact that his eyelids were continuing to function as usual. But regardless of his eyes, something needed to happen, Herr Faustini told himself. "In the end, who am I, according to Herr Faustini?"

He sat straight up in bed. "I'm not just that," and he pointed to the invisible, ugly clump lying in front of him. "I am…," at which point, Herr Faustini faltered, not knowing how to continue. The metallic taste of dreariness spread through his mouth, and every single word he had just now wanted to express failed him. Herr Faustini realized that the time for talking had passed. When conversation no longer avails, all that remains is action. On a day like this, naturally much is demanded. Much is demanded? There was no one left to demand anything from him anymore. Everything with work was now over. Herr Faustini did not have to go to the office, thank God… or perhaps that was unfortunate on a day like this? At the office, at least Hammerer would have looked over and started in on one of his typical Hammerer jokes, which Herr Faustini would have laughed at in order to bring Hammerer a little joy. Hammerer had always joined in laughing at most of his jokes, so hard that his stomach rippled up and down.

Since there was no one here to demand something from him, Herr Faustini now demanded something from himself: to get dressed and leave the house. He slipped into pants and shirt, tied his shoes, and set out food for the cat, which was nowhere to be seen. He walked to the bus stop and waited. The bus arrived right on time. Herr Faustini pulled out his railcard, and the driver nodded. Herr Faustini picked a window seat, and let the trees be trees and the houses be houses. As the bus rounded a curve and the lake lay flatly gray before him, Herr Faustini's heart grew a little lighter, despite the fact that it was one of those days. Herr Faustini breathed in deeply and whispered to himself: "It can't go on like this. I won't be beaten just like that." Herr Faustini's voice threatened to become louder. "They won't break me without a fight," at which point Herr Faustini almost got to his feet. "Starting today, my life will be an adventure, an array of tiny adventures, and even if they are itty bitty ones, they will still be my adventures." This is what Herr Faustini decided on this particular morning on the bus between Hörbranz and Bregenz.

As he stepped onto the pavement, Herr Faustini noticed that something was different. The train station was the same hideous station, but he himself, Herr Faustini, was someone else. His heart felt much lighter, despite the fact it was one of those days. Something inside of him had woken up, and Herr Faustini fought a desire to turn to the first person he saw, like the old lady with the purse over there, and hug her, and share with her that everything was now different. However, he let the old lady move on undisturbed and made his way into the city. "A plan, a kingdom for a plan," whispered Herr Faustini to himself. "A kingdom for a plan," he repeated under his breath, glancing to the left and right to see if anyone had overheard him.

Nobody. But wasn't having a plan actually the opposite of having an adventure? Therefore, onward without a plan! However, Herr Faustini was too cautious for this course of action. "A little plan," he murmured to himself. A tiny plan, Herr Faustini decided, if everything was to be different, then not just somehow different, but masterfully different. And as he sauntered toward the city and the office workers hurried past him here and there — it was not easy to resist being swept along by their urgency, to maintain his own quiet pace, considering that in the past he had spent more than enough time keeping up with the hurried office staff tempo — anyway, as he sauntered along, refusing to let his stroll be disrupted, it occurred to Herr Faustini that every new beginning had to be sealed by a visit to the hair salon, since a visit to the hair salon was much more than just a haircut.

The salon was completely pink, and over the door stood the word *Heaven*. As Herr Faustini opened the door, a small bell chimed. A young woman smiled at him out of her large eyes and gestured for him to take a seat in the salon chair. Herr Faustini settled down in it as if he had never sat anywhere else. The young woman said her name was Nicole, and Herr Faustini almost clambered down out of the chair to introduce himself properly, but instead he opened his lips slightly and said: "Faustini."

Nicole led him to the sink, and the warm water cascaded over his head, as if it had countless reasons to become acquainted with every centimeter of Herr

Faustini's head, as he grew too languid and drowsy to understand why. Just let it happen, Herr Faustini told himself, Nicole is washing your hair and just let it happen. How could Herr Faustini have known that Nicole's hands were not just the hands massaging his scalp? They were magical hands that transformed every centimeter of his head into a site of ecstasy. Herr Faustini did not exist beyond the hair Nicole was washing and the scalp she was massaging. Across a great distance, he heard Nicole ask: "Does this feel alright?"

He bobbed his head mutely, as if it were wrapped in soft cotton. He simply did not want her to stop. The scalp massage had to end eventually, Herr Faustini knew this, but he was willing to shove this knowledge far back into the dusty nether reaches of his consciousness as long as he could. The magical hands lifted from his head, and for a moment, he registered their absence as a chill in the air. But Nicole was already gently wrapping a towel around Herr Faustini's head, which she began to rub softly. In front of the mirror, her magical hands executed a series of movements that might have signified cutting, shaping, and styling. Herr Faustini perceived all of this from across the great distance created by the pleasure that still enchanted him. He nodded gratefully and acquiescently, while Nicole continued to work. The silhouette of the man in the mirror amused Herr Faustini, who did not associate this person with himself. Nicole modulated the man in the mirror, touched him, eyed him from all angles. Finally, she held a hand mirror up behind this head, and Herr Faustini realized that the reflected head was his own. "Do you like it?" Nicole asked, as her large, beautiful eyes bored deeply into his.

How could he be anything but thankful? After all, it was not every day that a man like himself experienced something like this, as the object of a lovely and courteous young woman's exclusive attention. Yes, Herr Faustini was very satisfied with what Nicole had created. In the mirror, he could see clearly that the head of this person, who was indeed himself, bore evidence of her efforts in the hair that was now missing from the places that it had once occupied. In the space where the old hairstyle had been, its absence was perceptible, an after-effect of sorts, and Herr Faustini could clearly discern this after-effect in the mirror. Without a doubt, the new haircut was more becoming, since it was the result of the efforts that the charming Nicole had focused exclusively on his head. Normally, Herr Faustini was not very particular about his appearance. He had entered Salon Heaven solely on a whim. In the end, a day like this one was comprised exclusively of a series of whims. The haircut was wonderful, mainly because it would remind him for a long time of Nicole's magical hands. The shadow of the absent hairstyle, on the other hand, would soon be forgotten.

Back on the street, Herr Faustini paused in front

of a shop window, and between the newest vacuum cleaner and coffeemaker models, he studied his reflection with its lingering after-effect of his old, now-absent hairstyle. It was a little chilly around his ears, and he only first felt at peace again with the new hairstyle when he thought back to Nicole's hands. He had just fitted his face perfectly into a shiny chrome cooking pot hanging in the window, when a large dark pink bundle swayed through the picture. Herr Faustini turned around and saw a dark pink bundle on legs walk by. He could make out a torso that began where the legs ended and, above the torso, the head of a young man wrapped in the dark pink bundle. With his spirits still high, thanks to his visit to the salon, Herr Faustini cheerfully approached the young man and asked him politely what he was carrying on his shoulders. With a smile, the young man stuck his head out of the dark pink bundle like a turtle and explained that what he had here was a parachute. "A parachute, indeed," Herr Faustini replied.

And in the interest of complete honesty, he added that, as a young man, he had longed to experience a parachute jump. As he said this, Herr Faustini thought he sounded a little too forward, and he fought an impulse to purse his lips, gaining control of his mouth in the nick of time. "There's nothing easier to do," the young man insisted. He could call the parachute club anytime he wanted and ask for Michael. He, Michael, would be delighted to take him along for a tandem jump. "Would you really be willing to do a tandem jump?" Herr Faustini burst out.

The blood rushed to Herr Faustini's head, not so much because he could visualize the free fall and the rapidly approaching ground, but because this seemed to be a day in which people were willing to talk to him freely and easily. Yes, this appeared to be a day in which his words were actually being heard and, at least momentarily, taken in earnest. A tandem jump together with this friendly young man with the pink parachute from 5,000 meters, with nothing above Herr Faustini except this very pink parachute and with the mercilessly hard ground rushing up from below!

Herr Faustini thanked the young man warmly, remarking that he didn't want to hold him up any longer, since he was sure he had more important things to do than to chat with him, Herr Faustini. He thanked the young man for his willingness and his offer, noting that he could have no idea what this offer meant to him, Herr Faustini. No, there was no way he could know. He thanked the young man again, and yes, it would certainly be worth calling the parachute club. And he wished him a good day. Herr Faustini also wanted to say that in his eyes, the young man was a hero, but the young man had already turned away, so Herr Faustini just whispered this to himself, "yes, a hero," as he stood on the corner, as light as a feather.

He turned around and saw a tall, very thin figure

in a tight, light blue outfit bending over the handlebars of a bicycle. On its head, this figure was wearing something that resembled a beehive. As the cyclist drove by, Herr Faustini was able to gaze into his eyes for a long moment. The eyes were fixed rigidly on a point unreachably far away. Reminiscent of some strange kind of grasshopper, the emaciated figure was perched on his sports bike, driving straight into a promising nothingness that was so alluring that no sacrifice was too great in its achievement. The gaunt figure's eyes were half-closed, as if in a trance, but they were not in the least bit unhappy. This person had probably reached a higher plane, and the rest of us who are excluded from it are the ones to be pitied, thought Herr Faustini.

As Herr Faustini resumed his stroll, mechanically skimming the prices of the latest razors, it occurred to him that people like the young man and the cyclist had hobbies, and that a hobby would perhaps be a good way to wake up in the morning and to not be faced with an ugly clump. A hobby could offer a way to get past such a clump, Herr Faustini surmised. He envisioned himself in a grasshopper costume with a beehive on his head, riding a bicycle with his eyes fixed on the beckoning distance. He visualized himself looking around with a hero's gaze and jumping out of an airplane, maybe even with a beginner on his back in a tandem jump. What opportunities and prospects there were in a totally different life! Nonetheless, Herr

Faustini was no novice when it came to the particulars of life. Even if he bought a bicycle, he doubted if he would take it out for a ride more than twice, and after the first jump, a pink parachute would vanish into his closet, falling into the section marked *Miscellaneous*. No, he had to stay as he was. Someone had to do that in this day and age, since no one seemed to enjoy their leisure hours in peace any more. Leisure was another word for *free time*, and free time meant being up on a bike, over in a gym, up on a mountain, or in the waves, until one reached an advanced age. Someone today has to stand up for the rights to be at leisure and, as far as I'm concerned, to be bored, Herr Faustini decided.

Although the small city of Bregenz consisted of only a few streets, all of which led nowhere in particular and then looped back around to where they had started, Herr Faustini venerated the high art of the leisurely pace as exemplified by the amble. In the company of his new haircut, he ambled proudly through the streets of the narrow city, making his way toward the train station. Every path and lane here eventually leads to the lake, but before you can reach the lake, you have to cross the train tracks. And of course, all train tracks eventually lead to a station. The old station had been demolished by idiots long ago, replaced by a noxious green monster of a station. They had posted the words TRAIN STATION every few meters along its walls, otherwise no one would have had any idea what this nightmare was actually good for. As if on autopilot, Herr Faustini's steps were directing him toward this structure. A little train ride wouldn't cause any harm, he assured himself. Fifteen minutes in the train, and the change of scenery would be complete. He would reach another small city in which, of course, there would be hardly anything to see or discover, but hardly anything was still a step up from absolutely nothing. Besides, train travel was, for Herr Faustini, one of life's finest joys.

In the station hall, a young fellow with a bold gaze was standing at a slightly oblique angle apart from all the others, most of whom who were oriented either horizontally or vertically. This fellow's gaze had a flickering quality about it, and there was something in the way he hurtled toward Herr Faustini that made it clear that this, at least, was an adventure. "I've seen you here often," the fellow remarked obliquely from above. "You come on the 78 and take the regional train to Bludenz, although you sometimes take the bus to Lustenau."

Herr Faustini valued human contact, however this specific contact lacked a certain sense of mutuality. Besides, his fellow conversationalist was rudely violating the personal space rule. "Yes, if you say so," is how Herr Faustini wanted to politely begin.

"Have you noticed that recently more and more people are riding their bikes along the station platforms?" the fellow continued. "Biking on the platform is strictly forbidden. I have repeatedly reported the infractions to the train dispatcher, but he has no interest in looking into the problem. That is one concern. The other concern is that the frequency of the trains between Lochau and Bregenz needs to be increased significantly. This would help alleviate the traffic congestion on the roads. During the Pfänder Tunnel closures, I recommend shuttle service at ten-minute intervals. The train should not admit defeat so easily. Anybody who has spent an entire summer stuck in traffic is ripe for rail travel. We have to take advantage of this. It's only a question of coordination. May I introduce myself? I'm an advisor for Bus and Rail VOL."

As he said this, the man pulled out a homemade name tag and presented it to Herr Faustini. He hurriedly added that VOL stood for *volunteer*. "If you have any questions about the timetable, ideas for improvement, or special requests, I'd be glad to take them."

Herr Faustini pointed to himself and said, "Faustini," as he extended his hand, but the fellow did not react. Herr Faustini let his hand sink, turned it over, observed his palm, and then tucked it away again.

"It's a matter of knowing everything at the same time," the fellow now whispered to him, "you understand what I mean? Everything at the same time." His eyes flickered, flared up, and shrank to half their normal size.

"Aha," Herr Faustini commented, as he glanced around for eavesdroppers.

The young fellow continued, "Who has everything in his head all at once? I'm the only one here who knows it all at the same time, do you understand?"

"I understand," said Herr Faustini. "Can you tell me if rail replacement service is going to be offered to Langen am Arlberg in the near future?"

"At this time, there's no replacement service in the works," the advisor for Bus and Rail VOL explained. "But if the weather is as crazy as it was the year before last, then a section of rail might be compromised at any time. Of course, that would require the rail replacement service to be activated, even it was just for a short time, you understand? They would have forgotten to include the ICE Zürich-Munich line, if I hadn't made a request."

"A request?" Herr Faustini inquired politely.

"Yes, I often make requests, sometimes just to see if they have anyone on staff who can actually think for themselves."

"And is there someone here who can think for themselves?" Herr Faustini asked.

"Yes, there's one person," the fellow admitted, "but what about when he's sick or on vacation or somewhere else?"

"Then someone else is here?" Herr Faustini answered uncertainly.

"That's me," the fellow replied, tapping his forehead. "Everything up here, all at once. I don't need a calculator like them over there. Everything's in here. Ask me something! Ask me!"

"What should I ask?" Herr Faustini asked nervously.

"It'll just come to you," the fellow assured him.

"It's not as easy as it sounds," Herr Faustini demurred. "You have to know the answer already, otherwise the question might not make any sense. If you don't know the answer, then you can't know for sure if the other person has gotten it right."

"You could be sure with me," the fellow said assuringly, as he tapped himself again on the forehead. "Everything's in here."

"Alright," Herr Faustini agreed. "If I take the regional train to Dornbirn right now and get off there, when will the connecting bus leave for Bezau?"

The fellow gazed at Herr Faustini in pity, as if he could hardly understand why such a simple question was being asked. "Every child knows that," he remarked. "If you leave at twenty-seven past the hour, then you'll arrive at forty-two past in Dornbirn. The bus to Bezau leaves at five past, so you'll have to wait about twenty-three minutes until the bus departs for Bezau. However, you could potentially take the bus that goes through Alberschwende..."

"No, thank you, I don't want to take the bus through Alberschwende. I also don't plan to take the bus to Bezau. It was just a question since you said I should ask about something, anything. You answered my question very nicely, congratulations. But I really just want to take the train to Dornbirn and then look around a little bit. When I'm done, I'll catch the train from Dornbirn back here. I'm a railcard traveler, you know."

It had been a long time since Herr Faustini had been so chatty, but he thought the fellow had earned it, since he was explaining everything in such detail.

"Surely you're a railcard traveler too," Herr Faustini commented, only to immediate regret it, because deep in the fellow's eyes something strange and eerie took place. His eyes began to change color, and something deep behind them flashed metallic. The fellow did not respond to the question, but instead his head pivoted swiftly to the side, and he hurried back the way he had come.

Herr Faustini had had enough, and it was still one of those days. He boarded the bus, which swayed him toward Hörbranz, while his eyes turned toward the lake.

-5-

The sun shone into the room and brightened Herr Faustini's mood considerably. Usually an easier day followed one of those days, even if the day in question ended up going well in the end. He looked around. The kitchen was submerged in a surreal light. The picture on the kitchen calendar had never looked lovelier than it did at this moment. A small pool of sunshine illuminated a single date. He was startled to see that in less than three weeks his sister would be celebrating a major birthday, which meant that he needed to find a gift for her. He rang Frau Gigele's doorbell. Of course, Frau Gigele had already been up for a long time. He was lucky that she was not running the vacuum, since otherwise she would not have heard the doorbell. Frau Gigele appeared with curlers in her hair. Her initial reaction revealed her embarrassment, as her hands flew straight to her head, but then she recalled the long years of their neighborly relationship.

"It's you, Herr Faustini," said Frau Gigele. "I thought it was the new mail carrier. I wouldn't want him to see me this way."

Herr Faustini was unsure if he should feel flattered or not. After all, Frau Gigele's comment implied that he was almost as good as family and, thus, allowed to see the curlers. Herr Faustini was uncertain if he actually wanted to belong to the family or if he preferred to be a member of the group of people from whom Frau Gigele hid her curlers.

There at the open door, Herr Faustini explained about his sister's landmark birthday and the fact that he needed a gift for her. His voice was so subdued that it was easy for Frau Gigele to perceive how heavily the gift conundrum was weighing on Herr Faustini.

"What have you been considering?" asked Frau Gigele.

"A potted plant," he admitted sheepishly.

"How will this reach her in Ticino?"

Herr Faustini had not given any thought to the transportation problem. Frau Gigele was right. The present had to be easily transported and deliverable by mail.

"What about a cosmetics gift certificate?" Frau Gigele inquired.

Herr Faustini would have almost hugged Frau

Gigele, if it had not been for the intimidating curler superstructure. Besides, she smelled rather strongly of hair chemicals. He departed with a lighter heart, set out the food bowl and fresh water for the cat, locked the house, and took the bus to Bregenz. He arrived in buoyant spirits, because now he knew what to give his sister. He headed straight to Helga's Beauty Salon, which he would now enter for the first time in his life. How often had he caught sight of the dark pink neon sign out of the corner of his eye? It is possible that this was the very moment that the setting sun caught its reflection in the shop window, which was inducement enough to look inside more closely. However, the secret goings-on inside the beauty salon remained hidden from the outside. Suddenly a single thought shot through his head like lightning: What would his sister do with a gift certificate to Helga's Beauty Salon, considering that she lived in Ticino? She definitely would not travel for hours just to visit Helga's Beauty Salon, when she could visit much more exclusive beauty salons in Ticino, even on a daily basis, since she had married well, cosmetic surgery consultations all inclusive.

Herr Faustini was back to Square One. The house of cards erected on his, and, more accurately, Frau Gigele's gift idea had collapsed. With slumped shoulders, he meandered along the pedestrian zone, from one optometrist's shop to another. The more glasses he saw perched on the faces of laughing models, the more helpless he felt. Could it be that Bregenz did not offer any real options in terms of gifts? But there had to be a present for Herr Faustini's sister in the city of Bregenz, despite the fact that she lived in Ticino and socialized in better circles. There had to be something that someone could send in the mail. A book perhaps? Music? Herr Faustini's sister did not celebrate a landmark birthday all that often, and for that, he was going to send her a book or a CD? He turned around and stopped once again in front of Helga's Beauty Salon. Surely he could find something suitable in here.

The bell above the door tinkled as Herr Faustini stepped into the beauty salon. Herr Faustini's nose went off in alarm. Yes, the concentration of oxygen seemed to have been seriously diluted in the face of scented oils and perfumes. The air hung heavy with scents that disclosed to him how rich the world truly was. Herr Faustini recognized instinctively that he was entering a world he never knew was out there, regardless of the fact that it had existed parallel to his own all along. Here he had passed into the universe of women. Here was their secret kingdom. Did Frau Gigele also visit the beauty salon? He imagined her allowing perfume samples to be sprayed onto the back of her hand. No, Frau Gigele did not really fit into the beauty salon environment. Frau Helga was cut from a different cloth. She moved like a queen, a secret queen, of course.

He looked around a little bashfully, almost as

embarrassed as he would have been if he had stumbled into a women's lingerie department. A woman, undoubtedly Frau Helga, wafted toward him with a smile, barely earthly in nature. It certainly was not like the kind of smile he saw among the novices he sometimes encountered on his walks along the Pfänder Ridge. Compared with the smiles of the novices, this one was a quintessentially worldly smile, although also enigmatic, liberated, Herr Faustini thought. Yet that was not the right word for it. She somehow smiled omnisciently, inspiring confidence within this kingdom of a thousand beauty creams. Herr Faustini briefly explained his situation, and, in return, he earned a benevolent and knowing nod along with a smile. Frau Helga knew what to do. A gentleman who did not belong to the same social circles was searching for a suitable gift. She cast a swift glance once more at Herr Faustini's jacket, one which had definitely seen better days. In light of that, the present should not be all too expensive. Without a moment's hesitation, Frau Helga reached down a bottle from the shelf. "This is a body shaping cream with skin tightening effects. It shapes the female silhouette, enhancing the skin's resilience and youthful élan. For the woman with high expectations in the prime of her life," added Frau Helga.

Herr Faustini was aware that Frau Helga did not mean it personally, but nonetheless, he liked her for using the expression "in the prime of her life." A more callous spirit would have been less tactful in describing the situation in which his sister now found herself, only a short distance from her landmark birthday. "For the woman who cares about her appearance, Shiseido offers an array of high-quality skincare products. Similar to the Purifying Invigoration Mask from Issima. Or were you thinking about a perfume? Chanel Nr. 5? Or does she wear something more subtle?"

As Frau Helga presented Herr Faustini with the various products, a curtain was pushed aside on the other end of the room, and a woman close in age to Herr Faustini's sister appeared, followed by a young beauty specialist. The woman's face reflected a deeply relaxed state combined with an expression of inherent satisfaction, the like of which Herr Faustini had last seen on a high school graduation trip to Italy on the face of an old classmate as he exited a prostitute's cubbyhole. Certainly, the comparison was not the most appropriate, and the woman, who had just indulged in the great joys of a cosmetic treatment, would have been quite indignant if she had known of the connection that Herr Faustini had just drawn. However, in her current state of rapture, it was unlikely that she was interested in telepathically investigating his thoughts.

Frau Helga continued: "For the nature-conscious woman, I have here an admittedly high-priced cream that promises miracles: *La mer*. It's the latest thing for nature lovers who value exclusivity."

Herr Faustini was already convinced that Frau Helga would have just the right thing for his sister. However, it was the certainty that, in the end, he would have to blindly select a birthday body cream for his sister that caused him to ask for a little time to think, since he was making no progress here in his deliberations. He excused himself politely from Frau Helga's hovering smile and left the beauty salon.

He walked along the pedestrian zone without really seeing anything. Like a child's rhyme, the words *body shaping cream* and *anti-wrinkle eye cream* and *Issima* and *Ticino* and *landmark birthday* and *better social circles* and *suitable for Ticino* kept twirling through his mind. Were Frau Helga's creams suitable for Ticino? Were they the latest thing in Ticino? Or the oldest of old hats? On things of this nature, Herr Faustini was completely ignorant, which he now regretted for the first time ever. Yes, he felt sorry for the fact that he had never been pampered in Helga's Beauty Salon, and never would be. Although it was not unheard of today for men to go for manicures and pedicures, even body peelings. Some even went in for cosmetic surgery. You heard about all these things, but Herr Faustini had never learned to actually relate to these latest developments, so they simply passed him by as if they did not exist. The women were no longer enough for the cosmetics industry, and a new market for men had been opened long ago already.

Indeed, criticism was one thing, but how far could someone really go with criticism? Had not his visit to Salon Heaven, not to mention Nicole's hands, been heavenly? And his day had been salvaged because of this visit, right? This was the unvarnished truth. Deep inside, Herr Faustini decided to bid adieu to the spirit of criticism in reference to all things cosmetic, and he was amazed at how good he felt in doing so. Then the face of a no longer young woman emerged from under an umbrella. Why carry an umbrella in this weather, Herr Faustini wondered. But before he could pursue this line of questioning, she began to speak: "I need two euros."

She looked at Herr Faustini as if he were responsible for finding a solution for this problem. This was due to the friendly look with which he greeted the world. How could this woman possibly know that this amiable gaze was not meant for her, but rather for Frau Helga, the mistress of over a thousand lotions?

"Young man," repeated the glaring woman under the umbrella, "I need two euros. This is not my usual way, but I am short two euros, and I need them right now."

Herr Faustini was undoubtedly flattered to be addressed as "young man," even if it only happened in order to create an indebtedness that had to be absolved through the transfer of two euros. A fair trade, Herr Faustini concluded. He pulled the requested sum from his wallet and handed it to the woman. The "Thank you very much!" with which she responded was so loud that it set him into brisk motion. The woman addressed an even louder "Thank you" to his receding back, and Herr Faustini felt as if he were being propelled forward by rocket thrust. It had been a long time since he had felt as light-footed as he did now.

Anyone who walks briskly either wants to forget something or has nothing that he could possibly forget. A brisk walk is not conducive to the recovery of a particular thought. Herr Faustini walked along quickly, until the point that he realized that his legs were actually functioning without him. What was it that he was not supposed to forget?

There must have been something about him that seemed to be an invitation. There was no other way for him to explain why the man with the hat spoke to him.

"Do you know Robin Hood?" the man asked.

Herr Faustini turned around and saw a friendly, smiling mouth and, above the mouth, dark eyes from which shone something that Herr Faustini could not name, meekness or cunning or alertness or something else. A basket was sitting beside the man, and in the basket, Herr Faustini could see two puppies.

"May I introduce someone?" the man asked. "This is Robin Hood," and he waved with one of Robin Hood's paws.

"Pleased to meet you," Herr Faustini said. He was about to give his name, when he paused. You never knew what someone who spoke to you on the street might want.

"Would you like to hold Robin Hood?" the man inquired. Herr Faustini was in the process of declining the offer, when he realized the puppy was already in his hands. How soft Robin Hood was! How warm this little puppy felt, cupped in his hands! Memories rose up within Herr Faustini, memories of summer days, of the sound of panting in his ear, of downpours and the scent of steaming dog fur. Herr Faustini recalled that as a child he had been afraid of dogs. Whenever a dog hurtled towards him, his breathing would falter. That was why it had been so nice when a dog let him pet it, wagging its tail and twining around his legs. Then Herr Faustini's world had been in good order. It had been as if he were suddenly drawn closer to the world. Now he was holding Robin Hood. Actually what he had been about to say was: I don't have the time, I need to get back over to Frau Helga's because of my sister. Robin Hood licked Herr Faustini's hand with his silken rough tongue.

"He likes you," the man said, and Robin Hood yawned.

Herr Faustini was touched by the fact that Robin Hood was yawning cozily in his hands, his eyes vanishing under a roll of baby fat. Who had ever trusted him blindly? The cat? He came and went as he wished. In reality, Herr Faustini was, for the cat, not much more than the cat food server. That's just the way cats are, especially the tomcats that had come over the years. Always acting as if they did not need anyone. And that probably was the way it was. The cat did not need him.

"Robin Hood is from Poland," the man with the dog basket explained. "I raised him. He only eats camembert with vanilla sauce," he added with a smile. "But that's why he's so happy!"

The man beamed a smile that was so contagious that Herr Faustini smiled back. Little Robin Hood, nestled in his hands, existed from nothing else except camembert and vanilla sauce? No wonder he yawned so contentedly with the roll of baby fat over his eyes. "What kind of dog is this?" Herr Faustini asked, studying the oversized fox ears.

"Robin Hood is a Welsh Corgi," the man declared. "The queen has twelve of them."

This is a very fine dog! Robin Hood is a noble animal, a sort of canine lord, Herr Faustini thought. I am probably not fine enough to hold such an aristocratic dog in my hands. With such a diet as his, he could not possess anything but noble manners. Such a canine lord is surely also well-behaved at home. He would not simply relieve himself in the house. Robin Hood blinked as if he would fall asleep there in Herr Faustini's hands. Total heartfelt trust, thought Herr Faustini. Who has ever had such faith in me? Would Robin Hood be a suitable present for his sister? She would certainly be delighted with him. Besides that, the daily walks would be good for her. She never left her house enough, and when she did, it was to run errands, not just to get out. It would be different with Robin Hood. She would have to go out, several times a day at that. First thing in the morning, too. What if she did not appreciate his gift? What if she was not willing to go for daily walks with Robin Hood? What if Robin Hood was a burden that she wanted to get rid of as soon as possible? And above all: Who would take Robin Hood to her in Ticino? More than anything, Herr Faustini wanted to avoid having to go to Ticino. He could not leave the house vacant. The house and the cat, not to mention the flowers. Speaking of the cat: If he brought the puppy along, what would the cat do? In revulsion to the new housemate, he would simply go on the run. It was still almost three weeks until his sister's birthday. The cat could not spend that whole time clinging to the top of the neighbor's apple tree. Oh, but he could! However, he would not, choosing instead to run away, and Herr Faustini would have to spend the evenings alone, dozing in his recliner. And what would happen with the canine lord on the train and the bus? Aristocratic beings did not typically make use of these forms of transportation. A canine lord would not even know yet that such things as trains and buses even existed. A dog like this would be driven to its walks in a state carriage. A little re-education would surely be possible, since the lord was still a baby, after all. A noble and spoiled canine lord baby, but the emphasis should be placed on the "canine" aspect, not the "lord" part.

All in all, there were more cons than pros where Robin Hood was concerned. However sorry he was, however much he wished to keep him, he could not take Robin Hood with him. With a heavy heart, he handed the puppy back to the Polish dog breeder, who touched the brim of his visor cap. Herr Faustini departed as quickly as he could, before he had a chance to reconsider his decision.

He headed straight to Helga's Beauty Salon. It was time to take care of the problem at hand. If he did not immediately acquire a gift for his sister, he would spend the coming days wandering from shop to shop, which for Herr Faustini was one of the most unpleasant ways to spend a day.

With its heavily laden air, Helga's Beauty Salon was now familiar territory for Herr Faustini. He confidently purchased the body shaping cream, and Frau Helga wrapped it in lovely wrapping paper. In the plastic shopping bag, she also tucked several samples of male cologne and creams, which he was supposed to keep for himself. She bid Herr Faustini farewell with a handshake and a sparkling smile. Helga's Beauty Salon would always be open to him. It was good to know that there was a sanctuary out there, in case Herr Faustini ever again found himself in dire cosmetic straits.

-6-

On the street, it seemed to him as if the city smelled somehow differently, somehow like cream and fabric softener. The scent grew more intense the closer his nose came to his jacket. Should the brief sojourn by Frau Helga have had smell-altering results?

With the scent of the cream still in his nose, Herr Faustini's gaze fell on the letters THE END on a dark blue background. Above this floated an American name. Along the bottom edge of the poster, the words KUNSTHAUS BREGENZ were legible. That had to be the new cube constructed from opaque glass, which changed color according to the weather and the hue of the lake. Since its appearance, Herr Faustini had been interested in the glass cube, although it had never occurred to him to enter it. Herr Faustini compared the date of the exhibition opening with the date on his watch. The two dates were one and the same. The exhibition would open in just a few hours. The last exhibition opening that Herr Faustini had attended had been for an old painter from Hörbranz, who primarily captured the lake's various moods in his very delicate watercolor scenes. The entire village had shown up for the exhibition opening in the community center. The mayor conjured up laudatory words for the sprightly hobby painter, who was then serenaded by a string quartet from the Hörbranz Youth Orchestra.

Herr Faustini decided he would take part in the opening of the American painter's exhibition. After all, a foray out into society would not cause him any harm.

Herr Faustini walked past the military swimming pool on his way home, dropped off the birthday gift for his sister, donned a fresh shirt, threw a quick glance into the mirror, and returned by foot to Bregenz, though not without his umbrella, since the leaden clouds in the sky boded rain. By the time Herr Faustini and his umbrella had taken up a position against the corner of a house across from the art center, the exhibition opening was less than an hour away. From here, he could observe the people attending the opening. Herr Faustini somehow suspected that, as an event, this opening would be quite different from the one connected to the exhibition by the hobby painter from Hörbranz. Gradually, elegantly clad ladies and gentlemen, mostly in pairs, began to appear, some of whom were soon sipping on glasses of prosecco in the art center cafe. The favorite color among the exhibition guests seemed to be black, which barely differentiated them from mourners at a funeral. Most of the women wore their hair up, reflecting recent fashion trends, but they were not sporting black hairnets, as had once been customary at funerals. It did not take long before Herr Faustini was able to tell from a distance which of the passers-by were going to the exhibition opening, because the visitors shared something in common. They somehow all looked unique, as if they had been inspired by something deep inside to correspond their external appearance with the experience to come, which was not all that simple to achieve, unless you happened to know ahead of time what you were going to encounter.

Herr Faustini had never before been part of such a gathering of conspicuous individuals, and therefore, it was not surprising that, with each passing minute, he grew more nervous from where he stood on the corner. The first drops of rain began to fall, and soon a steady shower developed. Herr Faustini debated whether it might not be better to just go home. The cat would surely value his company, even if he would be surprised by his master's new, slightly eccentric scent. What did someone like Herr Faustini have to search for at a major event like the one that was about to begin over there in the glass art center? However, what could actually happen to him there? Just this once,

Herr Faustini would take part in society life, and so on wobbly legs, he crossed the street and stepped into the glass building. Stretching all the way across the stark room, a net of conversations, thick and reverberating, surged toward him out of the semi-darkness. The space reminded him of a parking deck, only somewhat nicer, though he could not have said exactly what made it nicer.

Herr Faustini's first impression was that one thing that was different was the talking, which was like a net of self-assurance. A net that confirmed for the speaker that he actually existed and, more importantly, that the others recognized that he existed. There was no other way that Herr Faustini could explain the excited chattering of the speakers around him. In the end, there was no clear benefit that could be expected from this effort, since no one could really register the flurry of conversation. Herr Faustini was especially struck by the eyes, which were everywhere. They looked everywhere at once and were seen from everywhere at the same time. It seemed to him that these eyes were leading lives independent from those of their carriers, as they roved all over the place, unhindered. Herr Faustini stood there, his closed umbrella pooling a little puddle on the black marble floor, and had no idea where he should look or even go. He noticed the scrutinizing gazes that skimmed across him, and he nodded cordially in return, although there was no corresponding response in these eyes, which quickly turned away from him, perhaps because he was a blank page. An attractive woman smiled encouragingly across to Herr Faustini. She was, without a doubt, socially significant, as reflected by the fact that everyone around her was oriented in her direction like iron filings toward a magnet. Herr Faustini quickly proffered his most charming smile in return, which the woman graciously accepted, right before someone jostled his shoulder and pushed him aside. A burly man plowed past him, straight toward the woman on whose cheeks — left, then right, and then left again — he pressed his lips. She reciprocated each of these, although not really, since she did not kiss the man himself but rather the air that surrounded him. It had been a misunderstanding, a stray smile. Herr Faustini should have known. Herr Faustini was rarely in the position of not knowing where he should look or direct his feet. Or where he should conceal his dripping umbrella. He had not prepared himself for a situation like this. He stood helplessly in the midst of the exhibition visitors as they conversed to the best of their abilities and strew every imaginable scent around the room.

All of a sudden, the voices dropped, and all gazes fixed themselves up front, where a man in his mid-fifties, wearing a black turtleneck sweater, stood and greeted everyone there. The man's hair seemed to be separated into countless, small, twisted, damp clumps, which pointed out in all directions. Herr Faustini appreciated that anyone devoted to artistic things had to look the part. After the greeting, the man moved directly into a lecture, the like of which Herr Faustini had never experienced. Herr Faustini had been unaware of the existence of such words as *Manichaeism* and *meta-levels* and *palindrome* and *syncretism*. As he tried to deduce their meanings, he imagined meshes entangling him in the undergrowth of this lecture. He defiantly memorized these mesh-like words. Perhaps one day he would have an opportunity to get the drop on someone who had deservedly stumbled into one of these traps. The man in the turtleneck seemed to view art history, as well as intellectual history, as a general store from which he could serve himself at whim. At any rate, the man bubbled forth names, ones that Herr Faustini considered of dubious fame, followed by catch phrases, all of which were acknowledged by nods here and there. Even the blonde woman nodded at the appropriate spots, surely as an indication of her understanding. Herr Faustini admired the ladies and gentlemen in attendance here for the tremendous amount of erudition that filled this space, due the concentration of so many wise minds en masse. In comparison, he was a nothing and a nobody, a simpleton incapable of following even a single sentence. For him, the lecture by the man in the turtleneck was nothing more than an impenetrable sausage of words, from which he could not chew off even one bite. Speaking of chewing: Against the back wall of the exhibition space, food shimmered in green, yellow, and red. And there did not seem to be a dearth of beer or wine over there either. Herr Faustini studied the knot of people who had been frozen into listeners, and then looked back over at the buffet that had been set up. He detected a force field emanating from that spot in the room. It seemed to him that some eyes wandered with increasing frequency toward the table, where busy hands had set up the buffet.

With a magnetic gaze, the man in the turtleneck reached his final comments: "Only first when the transmutation of meanings is also subsumed into the material plain can the metaphysical mouse finally reach its cheese. I certainly don't need to explain to any of you that, for this center, this event represents a new zenith in its history of zeniths. We have been given the honor of hosting this exhibition exclusively as a world premiere, before it travels on to Paris and ultimately to New York. This uniquely serendipitous event here in Bregenz was brought about through the close, cultivated connection between the center's director and our artist, an acquaintance that reaches back over the years. It is now my pleasure to announce the opening of this exhibition by the great American artist, [Herr Faustini could not understand his name], who is here among us tonight."

The man in the turtleneck smiled as he gestured

expansively toward the artist, whom Herr Faustini tried in vain to catch sight of in the midst of the black-clothed spectators. The speaker nodded amicably as a hundred hands clapped their applause. The listeners then stormed the buffet, while a small circle of guests gathered around the speaker. He calmly accepted the praise offered to him with a ready smile on his lips at the appropriate moments. The attractive woman held out her catalogue for his signature. He protested modestly that all he had done was give the lecture, but yes. The attractive woman handed him a pen as she assured him that his talk had been splendid.

Herr Faustini moved cautiously toward the buffet. He reached between several silhouettes and picked up a glass of red wine. He did not risk eating anything, since he was much too excited for that. Besides, he might need to talk with someone, and a full mouth would not be conducive for that. Herr Faustini stood small among the animated, babbling guests. The general state of excitement was a new experience for him, since the people in this region were sooner known for their unflappable temperament. The excitement had to be tied to art and the things that surrounded it, as well as the talking and the being heard while talking that went along with the artistic goings-on. Up to this point, Herr Faustini had not seen any of the artworks, and it was time to change that. With his wine glass in hand, Herr Faustini began to hunt through the room in search of the artworks. His gaze meandered from one wall to the other. He could make out the outlines of missing light switches and soon ascertained where, in a worst-case scenario, the fire extinguishers were not hidden. Of pictures, there was neither hide nor hair. Except for himself, no one else seemed disturbed by the missing pictures. The people chatted, drank, and talked with their mouths full, as Herr Faustini averted his eyes out of courtesy.

Herr Faustini considered to whom he should turn at this stage of his search for the pictures. He could not approach the man in the turtleneck and ask: Congratulations on your talk, but please, where is the art? No, he continued looking on his own, since the pictures had to be somewhere. Far off in a back corner of the room, a strange tube made of glass was leaning against the wall. A group of people were standing around it at a respectful distance, as someone gestured and talked. Herr Faustini drew closer. The tube had to be the artwork. Herr Faustini could see this from the expressions of the people as they stood around and chatted. Within the tube, Herr Faustini could make out a neon sign, which bore the words THE END. The letters flashed on and then off. Perhaps a loose contact somewhere. Herr Faustini looked around, but no one else seemed to share his deduction. There it was again: THE END. Lips were pursed forward, a nod here, a tilted head there. So this was the artwork.

Herr Faustini studied the tube from all angles. THE END appeared and disappeared from the tube. Surely there was a deeper meaning concealed in the flashing on and off of the words THE END, something that Herr Faustini was missing. In the faces of the other viewers, he detected a lightness, a state of relaxation perhaps. Was it possible that they all knew the secret of the tube with the words THE END? Or did their relaxation actually stem from the fact that they did not really want to know the deeper meaning behind the words THE END? As Herr Faustini conceived these thoughts, he felt relief. Yes, that had to be it. They did not want to know. They felt comfortable in their ignorance, since knowing something with certainty is a sad thing. Herr Faustini had had to learn this over and over again. You hardly learn the why, wherefore, and from where before you are overtaken by a paralyzing sadness. Why was this? No more whys. It was simply the way it was. Accept it and that's the end of it! Despite his willingness to get to the bottom of the problem behind the words THE END in the tube, Herr Faustini found himself smiling all of a sudden. There was nothing else to do. He felt the deep joy that could be generated by an unfathomed concept. And he understood why all of these people had made the effort to come to the exhibition. They had to be so very grateful to the clever man in the turtleneck whenever he presented yet another artwork whose meaning would forever remain unclear. Yes, they hoped for nothing more than this: that the art would stay obscure to them for ever and ever. Because in obscurity, the not-knowing, they had discovered a great source of joy, possibly less discovered than actually felt. Thus, the demanding nature of art was transformed into a power, a joy. This explained the faces of the people in the beautiful clothes.

Herr Faustini, who until just now had been committed to seeing art as something strenuous, now grasped that art was one of the least demanding things in the world. However, because he knew how easily he exaggerated new things at their beginnings, he added "a little demanding" to himself. And then there was the fact that, at the exhibition opening, the joyous not-knowing was rewarded with food and drink. He found this simply... He did not know what he was supposed to think of this. If art was a glass tube with an appearing and disappearing neon sign in it, then anybody who searched for art and spent his evenings doing so was a hero. At least, these were his initial thoughts on the matter. Yet, now he realized that here everything pivoted around a higher law of joy, one that he had not been informed about previously. Whenever Herr Faustini was allowed to learn or experience something new, he was always filled with a feeling of gratitude. And this was what he felt now as well. If he could have had his wish, he would have hugged the man in the turtleneck, but he seemed too unapproachable, too redoubtable, for that. Herr Faustini admired this man for his cleverness. The man in the turtleneck had to be several people all rolled into one. He was not only a wise guide in all things art, but above all, his lecture about art had to be incomprehensible for every single person here, so that all of them could be inducted into the joy of not-knowing, which was the reason why they all came to the art exhibition in the first place. For those in attendance, evenings like these were of the highest order possible. When would they otherwise find an opportunity to experience such deep joy through not understanding anything of what was going on around them, while not risking any instance of harm, since ultimately all this here had nothing to do with anything? Buoyed up by this nothingness, they would go home with light hearts, where there was always something going on which would not allow them the luxury of incomprehension.

Herr Faustini was enthusiastic about his first evening in the presence of real art. Even if the smile from the attractive woman had been a mistake, he would carry it home with him as a souvenir, as he would the glances and conversations of all the other people here. Of course, he had not actually talked to anyone, but that did not really matter. He had shared with all of them something significant, and for this one evening, this had almost forged them into a kind of family. In thankfulness, as he left the art center, Herr Faustini bid farewell to each of the others with a friendly look. Outside he opened his umbrella and walked off like someone who had just made a breakthrough in an important matter, toward the silence of his house where the cat was waiting for him.

-7-

On his way to the bakery, the morning air caressed Herr Faustini's cheek so delicately that he paused to enjoy the gentle breeze. The air was seldom so uplifting, so velvety against his skin, and its tenderness reminded him of Robin Hood the puppy, which had nestled in his arms like fluid comfort itself. Some kinds of soft air passed softly between his fingers, like cashmere wool. Or like Robin Hood's warm coat. Who had ever trusted him as much as Robin Hood had? This question confronted him once again. How often had he secretly yearned to offer someone warmth and comfort, as well as security? No woman had ever entered his life. There was no why. When Iris — the then eight-year-old daughter of his sister, who had once paid him a visit while traveling through the region — had with innocent naturalness placed her hand in his and walked beside him, Herr Faustini had felt warmth flood his chest, as tears of joy sprang into his eyes. It had seemed to him that never before had he been so close to life itself, nor had he ever felt the heartbeat of life so acutely, as he did at that moment when the child's hand had rested in his. Back then, he had wished for a family for about an hour — or had it been a week? — one that he could take care of. But that had never come to pass. Hardly any women had ever been in his house. He figured the only ones had been Maria, his cleaning woman, and the woman from the gas works who had recently started doing the meter readings. Herr Faustini's family was the cat, which blessed him with slowness and warm evenings purred away in his armchair.

-8-

Sunday. The city was an empty swimming pool. A solitary, older gentleman crossed Leutbühel Square in creaky Sunday shoes, casting appraising glances to all sides. What made sadness rise in faces only on Sundays? Was there a general directive out there that kept missing Herr Faustini: Be sure to put on your sad face on Sundays, please! That had to be it. How else could the faces of the few walkers along the lake promenade — not to mention the sadness quota in the area around the train station — reflect the same empty, sad expression? Without exception, the Sunday walkers all presented the same face, which made Sundays especially hard for Herr Faustini. Furthermore, public transit practically came to a standstill on Sundays. Who took the bus or train on Sundays? Express travelers from Munich to Zürich, otherwise practically nobody. Herr Faustini viewed even the smallest stirring of zest, of normalcy, on a Sunday as a gift from the gods. A person with a lively face who refused to be consumed by Sunday's maelstrom… Just such a person was a bright spot for Herr Faustini, and the opportunity to spend even one minute in his company was enough to salvage the entire day.

The most elegant man on Lake Constance approached. Herr Faustini had frequently seen him out and about, always in double-breasted suits of various hues. One time his suit had been blue, another time violet, then brown, and the next time ochre. This man always twirled a short walking stick with an ivory knob, like a flâneur in an old French film. This man never looked at anything, or at least, he acted as if he was never looking at anything. Bored, the man chewed on his upper lip and gazed out across the lake, although it did not look as if he were actually seeing the lake. This man was black, and rumor had it that he was a prince from Africa. No one else sauntered along the promenade like he did. He hardly seemed to touch the ground. And since he barely touched the ground, there was a chance that he was not really here. Herr Faustini looked around for other witnesses, but none were in sight. More than once, he had toyed with the idea of saying something to the African prince. However, the prince moved in his own distinct light. A glowing corona accompanied him, belonging to him and him alone. It was impossible to talk to a prince like this one. He avoided all eye contact, but that could have also been related to the fact that he was not really here. And whoever was not really here was stranded within the sadness. Indeed, a great sadness engulfed the black prince. Herr Faustini recognized this, and he wanted to send a word to him through the palisade of melancholy. He put on his friendliest of faces and waited until the prince drew closer.

"Don't you agree that Sundays are boring?" Herr Faustini asked.

He immediately regretted his question. He should have come up with a better question or not said anything at all. The prince was startled, which may have reflected the likely truth that no one had ever asked him a question here before.

"*Oui oui*," the prince replied as he kept walking, "*le* Sunday is boring."

Herr Faustini had another sentence at the ready, knowing that if he did not say something, the prince would move on.

"But the lake is lovely, isn't it?" he asked desperately, as he watched the black prince with the most cheerful expression he could muster.

The prince turned back toward him and said: "Yes, the lake is *très beau*. But it isn't, *c'est ne pas la mer*, it isn't the sea."

A sad light flickered in the prince's eyes as he continued his stroll. Herr Faustini gazed after him in silence, since there was nothing more to say.

Herr Faustini sat down on the pebble beach near the military swimming pool and looked across to the other end of the lake. The German shore near Constance was barely discernable. It was more like a vision of land. The lake lay there like a wide, open bay, emitting its own radiance. Herr Faustini imagined that it resembled the sparkle given off by a bay on the sea. The lake did not extend out into open water though, as would be the case with a true bay, Herr Faustini concluded. The open sea must roll further and further out. On the other hand, everything here stayed static, since the other side of the lake had nothing different to offer than this side. This explained the distinct stillness around the lake. For some, this may have sounded sad or even a little dull, but Herr Faustini loved the lake for the very silence that emanated from it. Herr Faustini had never sensed more peacefulness than he did here, but it was a dynamic calm, not a deathly silence. It was a tranquility that breathed, a living silence, unlike the kind that descended over a section of forest after a wildfire. No, it was a quiet all of its own, a unique sereneness that did not need people but which gladly shared of itself, if someone was prepared for it. Herr Faustini was prepared, especially on a summer morning like this one. He sat and looked out across the water as smooth as glass, from which a limp sail rose as if pinned in place.

It would have been easy to sit there the entire

morning and watch, even the whole day. And then it would be evening, and the day would have slipped away like sand between one's fingers. To stay in motion, Herr Faustini thought, always in motion, because motion was the only way for windows to open up. And through such a window, you could see into the colorful world in which movement and stillness intermingled and created either a moving stillness or a still movement. But first stand up, determined Herr Faustini. See what the legs have to say, if they are capable of traveling anywhere. As he walked across the pebble beach, Herr Faustini thought, yes, there is no greater secret than walking, even if walking itself seemed to hide no secrets. What walking sometimes accomplished, though not always, could certainly be taken care of by the train. To simply drive away from a problem. In the evening though, when you returned, would the problem still be there? Yes, actually it would be, but it would look so different by this point that it would no longer be recognizable. Thus, in reality, it was no longer there.

Herr Faustini's thoughts floated hither and yon as voices moved closer to him. Herr Faustini turned around and saw a group of people standing together. Could it be that twenty, even thirty, people could all resemble each other, and that specifically these similar individuals would be gathered together in one spot? Herr Faustini looked closer. What seemed to link them was the way they were standing, as if they were all listening to a speech. Some of them had clasped their hands behind their backs, while others were studying the lake as if they were judging an automatic feeding system at a fair stand. These people were not wearing any sad Sunday expressions. Herr Faustini found this unusual. Two rather stocky men stood off to one side, their rounded stomachs covered by short-sleeved, sky blue shirts. They were both wearing straw hats and the same model of sunglasses. They resembled each other so closely that perhaps only by peeking behind their sunglasses could someone be able to tell them apart.

However, upon more careful inspection, Herr Faustini saw that the slightly portlier man was about twenty years younger than the other. They were undoubtedly father and son. The younger man was demonstrating something to the older man, his hands held out flat in front of him. His gestures were reminiscent of someone trying to fit a square object into the box it belonged in. The other man, slightly knock-kneed, had his hands clasped behind his back. Trying to dissolve the tour group's scraps of conversation within his inner silence, Herr Faustini realized that he had to adjust his position. He unobtrusively drew closer to the group. He greeted them politely, striving to make eye contact with every one of the travelers. In return, the entire tour group greeted him with a hearty *Grüßgottle*! Tourists from Swabia, Herr Faustini determined happily. The larger of the two men in sky blue shirts was still sketching hard-edged objects with his hands in front of the other's darkened eyes. Herr Faustini walked up and greeted them courteously, before asking if he could be of any assistance. The pudgier one, whose hands were still floating in the midground, turned his head a little dazedly and thanked Herr Faustini. He then returned to his remarks, which the other man continued to absorb as he had before.

"He had put the box in Isele's basement, his widow's that is," the younger man explained. "But he hadn't said anything to Isele's widow, who wasn't there. Because she was at the market. However, he also didn't go over to the neighbor's house and tell her either, no, he didn't. And then he just left, yes, he did."

The older man stuck out his chin and nodded.

"On the way home, he bumped into Schmelzer Klaus and had a chat with him. But Schmelzer Klaus told him that the whole thing with Isele's widow wasn't that easy. No, it wasn't easy at all. Mainly because her brothers were firmly convinced that her deceased husband had lied about the material from the doorframe. And that's why no one could say exactly how the wood had gotten in the box."

The older man pushed his chin forward again and nodded thoughtfully. "It wasn't easy at all," he said slowly, nodding gravely.

"And that's why," the younger man continued, "it's impossible to say who actually benefited from the whole thing. Since nobody has any idea where it is stored at this point. They all agree on this. On this, but on nothing else. Nothing at all."

"At all, you say. And if they all got together?" the older man interjected.

"You'd never get them all at one table," the younger man replied, as he lowered his hands. "They won't speak to each other anymore. Nono."

"Hmmm," rumbled the older man. "I would pay a visit in order to see if it would do any good."

The young man exhaled heavily and nodded. The older man lifted his darkened eyes to Herr Faustini and commented, "You have a lovely town here, yes indeed, a really nice place," and he nodded.

Herr Faustini thanked him for his complimentary words. "You know, we take our annual excursion to a different place each year. Our destination this year is Bregenz and Bregenzerwald. You have a really beautiful landscape here." And to confirm his observation, he nodded several times and added, "Yes indeed. You know, we're all tied to the agricultural machine industry. All of us, yes indeed. Yep, and this is our annual excursion. Tractors, chippers, hay machines, ventilation systems, food pellet makers, hay tedders, milking machines. You know what I mean. There's a lot of farmland where we live. That's why you need so many machines. That's right, isn't it, Peter?"

The young man was still holding his hands up in

anticipation of being able to resume his story momentarily. "Yep," he agreed.

He turned his darkened eyes toward Herr Faustini and failed in his attempt to conceal his impatience. He seemed to be holding something back, like someone striving to prevent the release of certain downdrafts when in the company of others. This is how heavily the resumption of his story weighed on him. Since Herr Faustini showed no signs of exiting the conversation zone, the stout man in the sky blue shirt picked his tale back up.

"Strange, that they don't realize that this is not the way it should be," he said.

"Most definitely," the older man replied, "even when you're used to such things. Yes indeed. It helps to talk. If it doesn't help, nothing will."

"Yes indeed," the younger man rejoined.

Herr Faustini slowly sidled away without attracting the other two men's attention. He strolled along the lakefront and listened out across the lake, where the silence was building its own spaces. He attempted to make sense of the story told by the stout man in the sky blue shirt, but he gave up with the feeling that he had developed a knot in his mind. Herr Faustini trusted the silence from the lake. He thought: The lake will tell me why the stranger put the box in the Widow Isele's cellar, while she was at the market. However, not every riddle that you encounter while out for a walk can be unraveled by walking. Walking always helped, but it did not always produce a solution. Unless the riddle happened to go up in smoke while you were strolling along.

-9-

The next morning, the mail carrier came by earlier than usual, and he rang the doorbell, which he only did when there was something that needed to be signed for. And there was never anything that needed to be signed for. Herr Faustini had been sent by registered mail a notarized notification about the death of a relative in Liechtenstein, who had bequeathed to him a modest sum of money. Herr Faustini felt ashamed that he had never really thought about this distant relative in nearby Liechtenstein, and had not visited him for decades. This relative had remembered him in his will, perhaps just to give an unexpected sign of life from the other side of the border — that of the country, as well as of life. Although the sum the deceased had bequeathed was small, this inheritance caused Herr Faustini a minor headache. Since this had happened to him so unexpectedly and did not fit into the normal routine of his daily life, he found that he could not make the decision to deposit the money into his own bank account. He wanted to deposit the money in a bank in Liechtenstein and take his own good time in considering how he could best use it.

It had been a long time since his one and only trip to the Principality of Liechtenstein. But what would bring him to this country, which had hardly anything to delight the eye except for the cruising of very expensive vehicles? And cars were not something that would have attracted Herr Faustini as a bus and rail traveler. Nor was Herr Faustini drawn to the principality by the steep view uphill to the royal palace enthroned high above the city of Vaduz, its painting gallery inaccessible to mere mortals. They said that this collection was comparable to the one in the Vatican. All he wanted to do was open a bank account in a Liechtenstein bank.

Without even glancing at its name, Herr Faustini entered the first bank that crossed his path, where he was greeted by a marble hall unlike any other bank reception area. As he gazed around the palatial space, mouth half open, his first impulse was to turn around and walk back out again. But then, right as he realized that someone like himself had nothing to lose here, a polite female voice asked if she could be of assistance. He now saw a woman sitting behind a tall marble console. She was smiling at him neutrally. Herr Faustini approached her and said that he had made a mistake, that he only wanted to open a bank account. But he seemed to have walked into the wrong place. The woman behind the marble parapet responded that neither of them could determine that. He would need to speak with Herr Ospelt, and with that, she pressed a button. A door in the middle of the marble wall swung open, and a meticulously suited man walked in their direction, extending his hand toward Herr Faustini. Somehow Herr Ospelt smelled of paper, and Herr Faustini wondered why Herr Ospelt's hand did not rustle when he touched it.

Herr Faustini had had no idea that in the Principality of Liechtenstein, banks were palaces. If he had known that, he would have worn his best shirt for this occasion. He felt Herr Ospelt's visual appraisal as a force that he was ill-prepared to stand up against. However, Herr Ospelt did not seem to register Herr Faustini's uncertainty. With studied neutrality, he inquired about Herr Faustini's request. Herr Faustini straightened himself up and asked with the harmlessness of the guileless: "May I open an account here?"

Herr Ospelt seemed relieved that the man standing across from him had succeeded in formulating his sentence. In an artificial brotherly tone, he answered: "But of course, you can open an account here! That's why we're here, isn't it?"

Herr Faustini nodded dubiously, while trying to maintain a natural expression on his face. He did not want anyone to notice that he had never really believed he could be successful in his efforts within these walls. Herr Faustini attempted to explain: "I recently inherited a small amount of money."

Herr Ospelt waved away his explanation, as if he really wanted to say: No need to say any more. You and all the other gentlemen in your less-than-best shirts always have small sums... Please, do not continue. Herr Ospelt gestured toward the elevator: "Why don't I go ahead and show you our vault right away? Please follow me."

Once inside, Herr Faustini could not figure out where the elevator buttons were located. Magical hands guided the car downward, while Herr Ospelt expertly straightened his tie. With careful nonchalance, Herr Ospelt commented: "I need to ask if you happen to be carrying a weapon on you."

In disbelief, Herr Faustini shook his head. "A formality, you understand," responded Herr Ospelt. Herr Faustini nodded.

Faced with the stainless steel vault, Herr Faustini felt smaller. Herr Ospelt proudly presented the vault door, as thick as a man's body, and invited Herr Faustini to take a look around inside, which he dutifully did. Lock box after lock box stretched one after the other, smooth and expressionless.

"Very discreet, isn't it?" smirked Herr Ospelt. "You can deposit cases of any shape and size with us.

Account deposits of less than one million Swiss francs are interest-free. For deposits over one million Swiss francs, the interest is 0.34 %."

Herr Faustini mentally calculated how many cubic meters of hundred-franc bills must be stockpiled within these steel walls. He kept losing count because he was trying to at least half-follow what Herr Ospelt was saying. There were places in the world that were much larger than the space within these steel walls, but down here Herr Faustini could clearly hear the throbbing heart of a world that he never knew existed. He was relieved when Herr Ospelt proposed that they go upstairs to fill out the necessary paperwork. Their elevator was lifted up by ghostly hands once again. The office was situated above the marble hall and commanded a green, bulletproof view of the area below.

"How much cash would you like to deposit?" Herr Ospelt inquired.

Herr Faustini was embarrassed, since he only had a fifty-franc bill in his wallet. "Are fifty francs enough?" he asked quietly.

"Let's say twenty francs," Herr Ospelt decided magnanimously. "Which other people, besides yourself, will be signatories on this account?" Herr Ospelt looked at Herr Faustini conspiratorily.

Herr Faustini did not understand what he meant. "Signatories? No one else," he said innocently.

"Are you sure?" Herr Ospelt asked with forced

casualness, studying Herr Faustini once more out of the corners of his eyes.

Herr Faustini did not have on his finest shirt. He absolutely was not a man who cut the best of figures in bank palaces. Herr Ospelt was accustomed to taking nondescript and obviously fortuneless gentlemen into the vault, where he watched them gaze around in amazement like children under a Christmas tree. And every single one of them opened an account in the most discreet bank in the world, naming at least one other man as a signatory. A man with a sonorous name, who did not find it necessary to come here in person, because he had better and more profitable things to do. The man with the sonorous name needed a lock box in the most discreet and tradition-bound vaulted nation in the world, and it was Herr Ospelt's task — and also his pleasure — to provide access to that lock box. However, the situation with Herr Faustini was different. Herr Ospelt's gaze still held a modicum of disbelief. Things really could not be as simple as they seemed in this case. After all, nobody except those seeking an impeccable hiding place for discreet gentlemen in the background were allowed to view the inside of the vault with Herr Ospelt. As a reward for this small service, the men in the less-than-impeccable shirts were permitted to catch a glimpse of the interior of the stainless steel vault, whose walls were thicker than their thoughts could even reach.

"We can always add additional signatories later

as needed, couldn't we?" resumed Herr Ospelt, continuing to watch Herr Faustini conspiratorily. Herr Faustini was relieved with this deferment of the problem at hand.

The papers were quickly set out. As Herr Ospelt put it, on discretionary grounds, no account statement address needed to be provided. As punishment for his refusal to name a second signatory, Herr Faustini was forced to take the elevator back down by himself. The woman in the marble foyer wearily bid him goodbye.

The Vaduz streets seemed somehow more familiar, now that he had the papers in hand that proved he was an account holder. Everything was indirect here in the Principality of Liechtenstein. Herr Faustini had always found it this way. The impression of indirectness came from the fact that everything direct was concealed under a thick layer of indirectness. This indirectness was the secret of the financial transaction world. Now that Herr Faustini had invested twenty francs in the local financial market, several veils had been lifted for him. The spotless cars gleamed in the sun as never before. The darkened windows of the string of well-signed trust companies glittered more powerfully than usual. Thanks to his involvement in the shared public secret, Herr Faustini even felt like he could relate to the young blonde woman sitting at the wheel of an over-sized SUV. He suspected that the people sitting at the wheels or behind the darkened windows or in the marble halls did not spend all of their time thinking about their complicity. However, it was the melody that led them confidently through their lives in Liechtenstein, as if the indirectness of life were itself only a joke.

-10-

Herr Faustini hardly knew how he got out of the Principality of Liechtenstein. It was like the blink of an eye and yet more complicated. He sensed this without being able to describe this transition in any kind of detail. This was because the trip back from the Principality of Liechtenstein was not just a short train ride, lasting less than an hour. It was a journey from another world with different laws and different faces and a completely different landscape suffused with a different light.

On the other side of the border, the train passed a stand of old fruit trees against which an old wooden shed leaned, like the ones that had existed long ago when Herr Faustini had careened through the meadows in short pants. The cars on the street running along the tracks had come to a standstill, but a silence infused by its own light surrounded the old trees. Such islands of silence had grown extremely rare in the Rhine Valley. They only existed in those places where it did not make sense to invest money, where the property owners had not yet heard about profits and yields. Where the islands were simply overlooked, ignored as if they did not really exist. Where they could stay and radiate their own light until the day came that a paper was signed, a transfer was authorized, a planning application was filed, a construction permit was granted, a demolition command was given, an excavator was driven up.

Herr Faustini could count on one hand the islands of silence he had seen, the ones he had walked through as if under a delicate veil that cooled his eyes. The Rhine Valley had been sold. The land was good money that could be converted into shining chrome Audis and BMWs, into Vorarlberg wooden buildings and homes, into Piz Buin Global stocks, into Threadneedle Growth Fund papers, into Kredietbank Luxembourg Equity Fund Europe shares, into Goldman Sachs Asia portfolios, into Gartmore SICAV Global Technology. In the winter, the land turned into weeks in Cape Town; in the summer, into weeks on cruise ships; in the fall, into hunt weeks; in the spring, into wellness weeks. The land was transformed into golf weekends, into truffle trips, into Buongustaio wine tastings, into special package ski trips, into gourmet weekends, into smoke from cigars rolled on the thighs of Cuban women and savored along with Barolo and business chitchat. This was the land that not long ago had been the land of silence surrounding old wooden sheds, on which elderberry bushes had once grown. But the times for silence were over. The land was paid for, the papers signed, the Audi purchased, the flights booked, the happiness achieved.

The telephone rang. It was his sister. She thought that it had been too long since they had last seen each other, and since her birthday was approaching, she wanted to officially invite him to her birthday party. At this moment, he heard, very close at hand though on the other end of the line, a plane preparing for descent. Yes, he could plainly hear how the engines were put in reverse thrust, as his sister carried on about a new restaurant that had opened up above Ascona and from which you could see the most gorgeous panoramic views. "You absolutely must come and see this new restaurant," his sister insisted, while Herr Faustini became just an ear, and this ear heard nothing except for the song of the plane as it made its descent.

Herr Faustini asked his sister to be silent for a moment.

"Why do you need silence?" she asked.

All he said was, "The plane."

"Which plane?" she wondered.

"The plane that is flying over your house," he replied.

"Over my house?" his sister inquired, before setting the telephone down on the small wooden table and going to the window, and then out onto the terrace.

Herr Faustini was alone with the plane, as it slowly sank closer to Milan. He could see it in his mind, like a heavy bumblebee bearing down on the airport, although if you were not too far away from it, you might think that it was drifting down from the heavens, so slowly did it seem to be flying. It is not that Herr Faustini wished to be sitting in that plane above Milan. Herr Faustini did not fly. Where would he fly to? Such a plane would fly across all the mountains within an hour. Herr Faustini preferred to travel through the mountains, to see the change in the landscape from village to village. No, flying was not for Herr Faustini. Those who flew overshot their marks. And no one could know exactly how long it might take them to truly arrive once they had gotten off the plane. With body and soul, not just with shoes and suitcase.

Herr Faustini stood weightlessly by the telephone. It had always been his wish to be in two places at one time. Now this wish had been fulfilled. And as is always the case when wishes come true, Herr Faustini felt like he was floating weightlessly on a sea of white apple blossoms.

At this very moment, his doorbell rang. Herr Faustini continued to float inertly. If he did not move, the disruptive person would have to move on. And Herr Faustini could continue to exist in two different places at one time. "Shhh!" Herr Faustini alerted his sister on the other end of the line, and she fell quiet.

Herr Faustini's ear hesitantly leaned far out across to the sky above Milan, while at the same time he listened at the door, behind which someone was clearly still standing. He pressed the doorbell again, as if refusing to believe that nobody was home. Perhaps he was one of those people with such an infallible sense of smell that he could detect the presence of a house occupant through three doors and five safety locks. In any case, Herr Faustini asked his sister to stay on the line for a moment, and he set the receiver down. He opened the door at just the right moment to shake the large, warm hand that was reaching out to him at shoulder height. A man was standing in front of him, and Herr Faustini had to throw his head all the way back to see his face.

"Hello, neighbor," the man said. "You don't know me, but I know you, and I also know your sweet cat."

Herr Faustini stood there with his mouth slightly agape. "Aha," he replied.

"We have been neighbors for a few weeks already, Herr Faustini, and I wanted to use this opportunity."

"Which opportunity?" Herr Faustini inquired.

"Well, you see, you have a shutter up there." The large man pointed up at it with an outstretched arm. Herr Faustini followed this outstretched arm, throwing his head back further and further, until he heard a quiet cracking. He had twisted his head as much as he could, but he could still not see what the man was talking about.

"And that's why I wanted to ask you if I could sort out your shutter."

"Sort out?" Herr Faustini asked.

"Straighten," the man clarified. "You have no idea what it's like to have to spend a whole day with a slanting shutter in your field of vision. I've been working over there in the house for several weeks now, and today I thought the time had come for me to just ask if I could."

Herr Faustini moved aside without a word, and the new neighbor bent down and passed through the door. He made his way unerringly toward the stairs and headed up, followed by Herr Faustini.

"Did you know that a slanting shutter like this can disrupt an entire day, from morning to evening?" He caught Herr Faustini's gaze and held it. "It is hard for me to accomplish much of anything. A slanting shutter like this both captures and devours gazes. It does not just consume your gaze, but it will go on to nibble away at your life."

The new neighbor opened a door. "This has to be the room," he stated. He went over to the window and opened it.

"See, here it is," he exclaimed, and reached for the

shutter, which actually was hanging a little askew, as Herr Faustini had to admit. The new neighbor extracted a tool from his pocket, tightened a screw, knocked so loudly on the shutter with his large hand that Herr Faustini flinched, and then turned back around, his face flushed.

"See, it's done now," the new neighbor affirmed.

"Thank you very much," Herr Faustini said, unsure what one was otherwise supposed to say in such situations. He suddenly remembered his sister on the other end of the line. The plane had probably landed already.

The new neighbor shut the window. Herr Faustini noticed his satisfied expression. The new neighbor exhaled deeply, as if he had just averted a serious threat.

"Paper stacked on the floor," the new neighbor explained, "a suitcase that is not put away right after a trip, empty wine bottles set behind the door, all of these things bother anyone with seeing eyes. That's how you end up going to hell in a handbasket," he remarked, "much faster than you'd ever think."

Herr Faustini nodded silently. He failed to see the takeoff point for his sentence. His sentence went like this: Neighbor, my sister is on the phone, please excuse me now. However, he did not see the takeoff point, since no gap opened up for his sentence.

"One time I lived next door to a stewardess," the new neighbor continued. "She always left her suitcase standing in front of her door. She told me it wasn't worth the trouble to put the case away. It was only two or three days before she would have to take off again. That did not sit well with me. There was simply no peace in that. She was disturbing the entire house by leaving the case by her door. Until I decided to go and put the case away. Finally, peace returned to the house. She rang my doorbell and asked about the case. I brought it to her and offered to regularly put her case away for her. And that's what we made off. I waited at the window until the light of the Fernet-Branca eagle sign came on. That always happened in the evenings around 7:30. My internal clock was synchronized with the Fernet-Branca eagle. It was so quiet in the house, since the suitcase had been removed from the door. And when the Fernet-Branca eagle lit up that winter evening, it was happiness itself."

Herr Faustini picked up the receiver and said, "Hello." But there was nothing on the other end of the line except the song of the plane preparing for its descent.

-11-

It had been a long time since he had sat so deeply in his armchair. It was necessary, in order to preserve a clear perspective on things. After all, Herr Faustini had two assaults on his life's previous orderliness to process. The words *Fernet-Branca eagle* still rang in his ears, and he decided that he would allow himself a glass of Fernet-Branca this evening. For cleansing and purifying purposes, obviously. He went to the kitchen and fetched a small bottle along with a glass. He poured the liqueur into the glass and drained it in one draft. He actually did not enjoy the digestif, but in difficult situations, it somehow helped to bring clarity. First to the stomach, and then to the mind. In the future, how should he deal with his neighbor — since ultimately it was a very familiar gesture to enter someone's home and sort out a shutter without being asked to do so? It was a violation of all the laws of acquaintance: to ring someone's doorbell, to push the homeowner aside, and from inside the house, to adjust a shutter back upright.

Herr Faustini had been so affected by this incursion into his personal space that he needed to warm up his insides with the Fernet-Branca. He could not really be upset with his new neighbor. After all, the giant had been engulfed by an aura of innocence and peculiarity, which immediately neutralized every bit of rancor. Instead of being angry at him, Herr Faustini felt a protective instinct toward his new neighbor. This man needed to be kept busy, since he was equipped with such a capacious amount of energy. Herr Faustini had realized that right away. A lack of sufficient engagement can have a disastrous effect on people like this, not only on them but, in this particular case, on their neighbors as well. What if, because of unusual weather conditions, he decided to dig up Herr Faustini's garden and chop down his apple tree, the one under which the cat liked to doze? The initial meeting with the new neighbor had left many things still open. These now needed to be maneuvered onto positive tracks. Under no circumstances did Herr Faustini want to leave the steering of their neighborly relationship to a bundle of energy like this person. He had to do something, to get to know the neighbor better. At best, on neutral ground. But he first needed to think things through. He had no intention of getting up out of his armchair until he had accomplished this. Because there was the other blow to his previous routine to consider: the invitation from his sister. However much he would like to see her — and however much he would like to see his now-grown niece Iris, whom he had not seen since that moment of incredible closeness between them, when she had tucked her hand in his (which for many others would not have been meaningful, but for him, it had been the moment the world came into being) — the prospect of seeing his brother-in-law, the chief physician and cosmetic surgeon, was extremely unappealing. Whenever he was with him, his brother-in-law's eyes never contained anything but disdain, and to be in that man's own territory would make it all the worse. Of course, he could not hold his sister's choice of a husband against her, but at the same time, it was undeniable that because of her decision, the once very close relationship between the two siblings had grown distant over the years. He would marshal his strength. He would give up his secure routine for her and leave his world behind. She was having a birthday, and she wanted to see him, in her own home. She was demanding a sacrifice. She knew what she was asking of him, since she still knew him as well as she did. She was worth every sacrifice.

-12-

Herr Faustini was afraid. There was no turning back from the trip to his sister's birthday celebration. He had to go, since he wanted her to see him as more than a cold, indifferent person. These were days of farewell and mourning. His house had never been so pleasant, his garden so unique, his cat so wise. The lake had never sparkled with such pristine blueness. It was now at hand: Herr Faustini was taking his farewells. Farewell to the world here. Farewell to life. What was he supposed to hold on to? Life was ultimately nothing more than a stage covered in invisible trap doors and danger zones. And why would anyone even try to keep himself safe? It could all end tomorrow under the wheels of a delivery truck. Herr Faustini saw black. He not only envisioned the approach of his own end, but the end of the world as he had always known it, which was also just around the corner. The days of protracted time were now a thing of the past, as were the long moments of gazing into the tall meadow grass, where the cat liked to hide.

-13-

Herr Faustini was in a real mental bind, so he went to Lustenau and strolled along the Rheindamm, as he often did in difficult times. A strong wind blew up high along his path. He walked against the wind upstream, and thought that he could hear voices. The wind was carrying moments from distant places that had once belonged to other people, although there were also untended thoughts in the mix. Here along the river, these had all the space they needed. He moved through the laughing and weeping of strangers as if through their living rooms. He let the others' lives brush his cheeks, although he really had enough to take care of in his own life. His thoughts gained momentum as he walked upstream. Many things simply thought themselves on strolls taken upstream, cobbling together solutions for nearly unsolvable problems. When he reached the point when his mental flywheel had made enough rotations, Herr Faustini turned around.

Moving downstream, the previously agitated and swirling thoughts settled back down. Nothing calmed Herr Faustini more than walking downstream. However, Herr Faustini walked upstream one more time, his eyes fixed on the Swiss mountains, where they piled themselves into a towering wall on the other side of the Principality of Liechtenstein. Beyond them were Ticino and his sister. He was supposed to travel there, to conquer this tremendous wall of mountains to reach the unknown. This trip presented the possibility that nothing would stay the way it had been. Once he left behind the radius of his world, anything could happen, as far as he knew. And it was this that he feared, the fact that everything might change.

A man's voice close to his ear tore him out of his thoughts. A man in an old military jacket stood in front of him, his hood pulled up over his head. He said hello to Herr Faustini. And after the word *hello* came the question: "Do you perhaps have any euros?"

Herr Faustini answered precisely: "We all have euros these days. Except for the Swiss, of course," he added.

The stranger was not satisfied with this information. He honed his question: "Do you perhaps have two euros you could give me?"

Herr Faustini admitted with regret that he did

not have his wallet on him. He never took his wallet along on his walks, since the wallet disrupted the free flow of his walk-related thoughts. The stranger accepted this with a sad nod. Herr Faustini wanted to resume his walk, but the stranger then said: "I have problems with your Witnesses here."

Herr Faustini asked politely what he meant by that.

"The Jehovah's Witnesses are quite annoying," the stranger clarified.

Herr Faustini did not know what to say, but the stranger continued: "In Israel, they gave God a different name a long time ago. It doesn't matter to me. It's all the same to me. But apparently not to the Jehovah's Witnesses. Besides, when you consider that they come from America, from San Diego as I heard, and San Diego is home to the largest American military base. Pearl Harbor and such. It was all agreed to. I mean, they can read newspapers from space with satellites today. I mean, they can see us down here and can probably read our lips, too. Yes, they're definitely able to do that. And they've created an artificial wind, not like the real wind here."

And the stranger lifted his right hand, stretching his pointer finger into the wind to test it. "Then again, what can you believe these days? No, this one is real, at least I think it is. They can produce an artificial wind that doesn't make any sound, just like that. And then they project an oversized slide over here, and we see what isn't really there. Have you ever heard of a Fata Morgana? That's exactly how it works. They project another world right here, one that doesn't really exist, and we sit here and watch television without the television, understand? The Jehovah's Witnesses are right in the thick of it all. They have such clean hands [he held out his hands], much cleaner than mine. But they will put us into a deep sleep, and we won't notice a thing. They have everything they need for this. The Fata Morgana is already programmed. While we've been standing here, it's started. Watch out! Don't believe anything! They're all around us, here in particular."

The stranger pointed, gesturing with a secretive, circular motion. Herr Faustini turned toward where he was pointing. "Watch out," the stranger said, extending his hand as if in farewell.

Herr Faustini moved to shake the stranger's hand, but he jerked it back. The corners of his mouth twitched as if he were laughing inside: "You can never know! They're everywhere! They just keep causing more and more problems. They won't get me again! Never!"

The stranger coughed drily and headed downstream.

Herr Faustini watched him go. That was the danger of going for a walk out in the open: At any moment, you could run into someone who just made you confused. The only thing that would help was to keep walking. Upstream, so the flywheel could gain momentum again. However, although the stranger was walking downstream, his mental state was clearly agitated. His internal flywheel actually should have been calming down as a result of going downstream. Herr Faustini did not want to catch the stranger's disquiet. Such a profound uneasiness, like that carried around by the stranger, was easily spread to the first person it encountered. And then he could pass the fretfulness on to the next person, and that is how it would go until everything spiraled out of control. Only one thing could counteract this: to remain calm, walk upstream, and look around. Look over into Switzerland.

There was no particular appeal to looking at the river, although you could not really ignore it. This river had been straightened a century ago, and now it flowed, straight as an arrow, into Lake Constance. It no longer flooded Lustenau and the other villages, but it also no longer gave off any power these days. It was as if the river spirits had vanished. The river spirits, Herr Faustini thought, now dwell in small rivers where only a little water still flows. The large, powerful rivers have all been tamed. They might be protected from flooding, but the areas around the large rivers are now dead. Herr Faustini imagined the meandering Rhine as it must have been over a hundred years ago, when it carried the springtime snowmelt from high in the mountains and rose beyond its banks. After the water receded, endless mudflats remained behind. No, that was no idyll. But the leisurely meandering of the river through the dappled shadows of the trees, as he knew from the small Laiblach River, this was an image that made his chest come close to bursting. The Rhine's source was located high up in the mountains. He would pass close to this point when he traveled to Ticino, following the river as he had always wanted to do.

As Herr Faustini had heard himself say time and time again: "Stay close to the rivers. Without rivers, there is no good fortune." Even if the river is actually no more than a channel, straight down which the water gushes to the lake, where it deposits thousands of tons of excavation material and silts up the lake. Unless the Rhine is renaturalized. But this really is nothing that Herr Faustini can cope with. He has other things on his mind.

The departure was really an imposition on his part. He would be leaving behind an unoccupied house with an emotionally needy cat, as well as two delicate flowering plants, which like the cat had never been left on their own before. Nonetheless, the trip had to happen. After all, this was his only sister, and it was not every year that she celebrated a landmark birthday. He struggled with himself over an excuse, contemplated one splendid hindrance after the other, but each of them collapsed upon closer consideration. A sudden illness which could befall anyone at any time? Herr Faustini never got sick. Only those who had someone to take care of them got sick. Regardless of how endearingly the cat brushed against Herr Faustini's legs, he could never play nursemaid. An appointment that could not be postponed as a reason for not going. Herr Faustini's sister knew all too well that there were never any appointments that could not be postponed in her brother's life. There was not anything that even resembled appointments in his life. An unforeseen event, an accident, a century flood around Lake Constance, an emergency situation after just such a catastrophe. (Hadn't two planes collided recently over the other end of the lake, and hadn't the debris from this accident plummeted ten thousand meters down to the earth? How easily a disaster like this could occur above Herr Faustini's house, in which case he would not be able to travel to his sister's birthday celebration!) No, none of these excuses would stand up under his sister's intense scrutiny. It was pointless, he had to go.

Herr Faustini had walked far enough upstream. Now he wanted to quiet back down. He turned around and strolled along the Rheindamm in the opposite direction. It seemed as if he was placing his feet into the still-visible loops of the footprints he had already left behind. As if he were collecting the loops from his footsteps, sewing them together, and closing their open ends. One more glance over at Switzerland, and then no more, as if it was not really there. And further back downstream, and into the calm and into the powerfully rushing water. The walking turned into a striding downstream, and then the striding became a floating, a gliding, a flying.

-14-

Frau Gigele, who lived with Herr Gigele in a small house next to Herr Faustini, looked a little incredulous, when he told her about his travel plans. Ultimately Frau Gigele could not recall Herr Faustini ever going on a trip. However, she was prepared to feed the cat, in addition to watering both of the delicate flowering plants every other day during his absence. Everything was settled. Herr Faustini was amazed at how quickly his travel bag was packed. This was because Herr Faustini never traveled (and thus had no idea of what a traveler actually should pack), and so he tucked only the bare essentials in his travel bag. In terms of what should qualify as the bare essentials, there are admittedly as many definitions as there are individuals who could be asked this question. The main thing was that he did not forget the body shaping cream for his sister's silhouette. That was the most important thing.

He was familiar with the railroad timetable, though he had never had a need to look up a train with a foreign destination. That was the reason why he called the train station and asked about the connections to Ascona. Yes, Ascona, Switzerland. Herr Faustini was startled at how quickly it went. He imagined the friendly woman at the information counter smoothing out the pages of the timetable book, while in actuality all she did was enter the name *Ascona* into her computer that then listed out for her the connections, including route variations and platform numbers. Bregenz-Zürich (thirty-minute layover), Zürich-Bellinzona, Bellinzona-Locarno. And from there, one would need to take a short bus ride to Ascona Posta.

"There isn't a train station in Ascona?"

"No, there isn't," explained Frau Judith Robatscher, who had previously introduced herself on the telephone with her full name and the question, "How may I help you?"

What besides train information could she typically expect to be asked about? And what was always sought were the fastest connections from one location to another. Yet Herr Faustini wanted more specific information. Not only more specific. He wanted different information. After all, the information personnel of the Austrian Federal Railways had all completed a training course. His call was answered after a not-too-long hold time, which generally included greeting customers with music and a recorded message, and then a return of the music followed by a request for patience and the assurance that the call would be answered in the order in which it was received. This not-too-long hold cycle had been abbreviated when Frau Judith Robatscher answered the call by giving her full name and asking, "How may I help you?" Naturally, Herr Faustini also introduced himself with his name. "Faustini," he declared, and cleared his throat.

He had not anticipated that he would need to present himself as an individual to the rail information person. It's all for the best, he decided. Frau Judith Robatscher should know who was traveling. Furthermore, once he had publicly shared his travel plans, there was no turning back. Herr Faustini wanted to know if there was a train connection that went straight south. From Bregenz straight south. Like the route that had been used for centuries by the merchants who had traveled across Chur along the notorious Via Mala, up to San Bernardino and then steeply down into the valley to Bellinzona. And not only merchants. It had been the mercenaries who had streamed past Chur in large numbers throughout the centuries, marching along the Via Mala and then up into the raw heights of San Bernardino. They had been hirelings of the Italian warlords, who paid good money for the services of these warriors with their long pikes. Herr Faustini wanted to know if there was a route that could take him to Ascona through Chur. Frau Judith Robatscher determined that yes, there was a connection through St. Margrethen to Chur. From Chur, he would have to take a bus to Bellinzona, and then board a train to travel from Bellinzona to Locarno. From Locarno, it was only a ten-minute bus ride to Ascona Posta. All told, the trip along this route would take over ten hours.

"Then I will take this route," Herr Faustini decided.

Frau Judith Robatscher told Herr Faustini that he might want to consider the fact that by taking the other route, he could reach Ascona in only six hours. This would result in a savings of over four hours. Herr Faustini asked Frau Judith Robatscher what she would personally do if she had available to her an extra four hours. Well, personally speaking, Frau Judith Robatscher concluded, she would use the four hours to go shopping. Or to go to the movies. "You understand, right?" Frau Judith Robatscher remarked.

Herr Faustini understood perfectly. Aimless wandering was one of his specialties. However, he had never roamed aimlessly through a totally unknown city. That could take a completely unpredictable turn. For example, a four-hour stroll through the city of Bellinzona or the city of Chur could end with him not being able to extricate himself from one shop window or another, whether it be a men's clothing shop, an electronics shop, or a cosmetics shop, which Herr Faustini now involuntarily knew a little something about because of his sister's birthday. The reason behind Herr Faustini's potential inability to free himself was not related to any particular longing to possess all of the objects contained within the windows. It was much sooner connected to his only half-conscious yearning to not have to leave behind the objects he saw before bringing them into some kind of internal order, so that they could be halfway free from care.

"Because even seemingly inanimate things carry a deep longing to be placed in some kind of order, don't you think, Frau Judith Robatscher?" Herr Faustini inquired.

Frau Judith Robatscher was silent as she took a breath, and then she was silent for a second, followed by a third. Herr Faustini rapped lightly on his phone receiver. Perhaps he had been disconnected.

"Frau Judith Robatscher, are you still there?" Herr Faustini asked.

"Yes," murmured Frau Judith Robatscher as if from within the silence of a cool cave, the kind you like to retreat into on especially hot days if one can be found nearby. Most of the time, though, on especially hot days, there are no cool caves close at hand.

"You want to take the bus from Chur to Bellinzona, right?" Frau Judith Robatscher inquired.

"That's correct," replied Herr Faustini. "Because, you see, Frau Judith Robatscher, the four hours that I will be spending traveling between heaven and earth with a view into the cool mountains will not be lost. On the contrary, these hours spent on the bus between heaven and earth will be unlike anything else in the world. Especially because I'll have no real idea of where I am. The not knowing where you are is a specific prerequisite for hours unlike anything else. Frau Judith Robatscher, I'm telling you this as someone who actually never takes a trip and yet is constantly traveling, if you can apply the word *travel* to those excursions you make even in the smallest of potential radiuses. Yes, I'm a traveler in miniature, Frau Judith Robatscher, and a passionate one. I travel every day and in the smallest radius possible, so that no one will notice that I'm traveling again. Well, there would be no one to notice that I was traveling except for my cat and my neighbor, Frau Gigele. However, tomorrow I'm going on a real trip to Ascona, for my sister's birthday. The trip cannot be postponed any longer, I have to go. I have put my sister off for years now, but that won't work anymore. What do you think, Frau Judith Robatscher?"

Frau Judith Robatscher said that she actually had no opinion on this matter whatsoever. Her sphere was solely limited to supplying information about travel dates.

"And are you content with supplying information about travel dates?" Herr Faustini asked.

"This rail information job is a job like any other," Frau Judith Robatscher replied. "Someone has to do this job, otherwise we will be completely replaced by computer-automated systems. People need human contact, and that is what I've been trained for."

"I did not mean to ask a question that was too personal, Frau Judith Robatscher," responded Herr Faustini. "Please excuse my impertinence."

Frau Judith Robatscher explained that he had not asked her anything that was too personal. Actually it had been the opposite. It was very interesting for her to finally have a caller who did not just want the fastest possible train connection. She had never had a caller who had asked for anything but the fastest possible connection.

Herr Faustini said goodbye to Frau Judith Robatscher, thanking her for her precise information before hanging up. He had definitely earned a Fernet-Branca. Now things with the trip were finally serious. And Herr Faustini was astonished by his courage. And whenever astonishment and courage are the points at hand, then a Fernet-Branca is absolutely in order. The Fernet warmed his throat. It occurred to Herr Faustini that he had talked Frau Judith Robatscher's ear off. Should he perhaps call her back and explain that he normally didn't talk so much? He poured himself another Fernet-Branca and raised a toast to Frau Judith Robatscher's well-being.

-15-

It went by quickly. Herr Faustini was already standing on the train platform. He had promised Frau Gigele that he would be back in three days' time. And the cat needed fresh water every day, and Frau Gigele assured him that she would take care of everything and that he could stay away longer, now that he was finally going on a trip. Now he was sitting on a train that smelled nothing like the local trains. This came as no surprise, though, since this was a Swiss train. Herr Faustini sat differently on this train, looked out at the foreign landscapes from a new angle. St. Margrethen-Chur. The approach up the mountains was dark — they were keeping the Principality of Liechtenstein to his left, piled one on top of the other like a wall. The train quickly reached the Chur station. Herr Faustini had no time to explore Chur, since the bus was already waiting.

Via Mala was as dark as its reputation. The gorge was so narrow that Herr Faustini could not help admiring the road that cut through this needle's eye. To be more specific, he admired the builders of this road, and he recalled old engravings depicting carriages traveling along the dizzying road built through the rock wall. Herr Faustini wrapped his fingers around the handle attached to the back of the seat in front of him. He sat straight up and let himself be carried deeper and deeper into the mountains.

As the bus exited Via Mala, it was as if someone had pushed aside a heavy curtain. Herr Faustini sat in this other light as it grew stronger and stronger, the higher the bus climbed. Up near the pass, the light was so clear that it seemed to Herr Faustini as if it were flowing like a breath across his mind. His gaze flew far out toward the south. For the first time ever, Herr Faustini was overcome by a yearning for the distant horizon, which struck him as more alluring than anything he had ever seen before. The bus passed a mountain lodge in front of which sat the famous mountain man, the one who was featured in the chocolate advertisements on Swiss television. In this light up here, Herr Faustini would not have been surprised to see the legendary Jürg Jenatsch himself, climbing the face of the mountain. And in his thoughts, he also greeted William Tell and his shouldered crossbow like an old friend.

The bus was already snaking its way down the

steep serpentine route into the valley, drenched in its own incomparable light. It was as if the light was emanating from deep inside of things. The colors glowed so deeply that Herr Faustini regretted that he had no sunglasses with him to protect his wide-open eyes. Sunglasses? Who in Herr Faustini's country has ever needed sunglasses? He had not owned sunglasses for many years. That had been back when he went skiing in the winter, and the snow had reflected the light so strongly that it had hurt his eyes and he had bought the sunglasses. How long ago had that really been? And what had happened since then? Herr Faustini cringed as he thought about the years that had rushed by since then. In a flash, they had sped past him, day after day, as if not even one of them had actually existed.

Here in the slowly swaying bus, it seemed to Herr Faustini as if a large wheel was turning backward, and as it turned, gaps were opening up. Only the spaces between the meanings had a shape, and the meanings were everywhere. The gaps were the means to fill the time. When walking, when being jostled around in a bus, and especially when waiting, the meanings fell away, like the shriveling leaves on a tree. Because everything was laden with meanings, which it wished to shake off. Meanings were generated through speed, an attribute that had become its own distinct value. First and foremost, speed meant the accelerated turnover of goods. The accelerated turnover of goods meant, above all, a reduction in breathing space. Reduced breathing space was nothing other than oxygen-poor lives that had been flattened by Audis and BMWs that had just rolled off the assembly line. Meaning was the current that pulsed within the temporal curve, that overfilled the minutes of every individual life until each person began to turn around in circles in search of themselves. The cyclical searches for the self began whenever it was no longer self-evident that the empty spaces were bursting at the seams with the garbage of meaningfulness, whenever the dead minutes became extinct, whenever each meaning came back around to itself. Nothing was self-evident any longer. Each gap cried out to be filled up, like the last of the old meadows in the Rhine Valley, which he had just left, the ones with the wooden sheds and the apple trees. These had finally been filled up, incorporated into the overall financial and commercial marketplace.

Herr Faustini was definitely digressing. Yet wasn't it the privilege of travelers to be able to digress? Along with waiting, wasn't traveling one of the last opportunities for digression? Waiting has been declared to be dead time, an empty space requiring filling. Red pens were already busily getting rid of these temporal and spatial gaps. Herr Faustini sat and waited in the certainty of having a valuable commodity to manage: empty, ownerless time which nobody except himself had a use for. The minutes that circled around him filled

Herr Faustini with a deep contentment. Who had ever had the happy experience of indulging so completely and totally in emptiness, as he was now doing? He was a time thief hoarding undiscovered, empty time, and he would sit on this trove and be nourished by it until he was satisfied.

-16-

Herr Faustini stepped dazedly from the bus in Bellinzona. Bellinzona, which sounded from far away somehow familiar, as if he had once dreamed this name. Was there anything that couldn't take place in a town with such a name as Bellinzona? There was no time for Herr Faustini to marvel at the palm trees, since the train to Locarno was already waiting. So much casual beauty along the wayside. A couple of excited breaths, and Locarno was already there.

The bus was waiting in the square in front of the train station. White sails marched erect across lake. The lake breathed with such deep blue sighs toward Herr Faustini that he had no idea what he was supposed to do with so much happiness. Herr Faustini suspected that behind the harmless word *travel* lurked an endless array of completely indigestible impressions that could carry him to emotional heights, the likes of which he had never experienced. The bus door slid open with a hiss. Ascona Posta. Herr Faustini blinked as he descended to solid ground. Something warm and sweet wafted up to his nose. The world here smelled so good that, for a moment, he closed his eyes. A soft pat on his shoulder. Herr Faustini opened his eyes. His sister stood before him, her eyes the color of lake depths. She tapped him appreciatively on the shoulder, since after all, he had done the unimaginable and was here. It was a short drive, uphill all the way. His sister's house commanded a view across the elongated Lago Maggiore. She led him to a room with roses growing outside the window. It was to be his for however long he stayed. She showed him the bathroom and hand towel. "Freshen up," she said, leaving him by himself.

Herr Faustini was moved. Everything here touched him, the view from the window through the trailing roses was its own revelation. He never could have prepared himself for so much beauty. This much loveliness was almost dangerous. Herr Faustini smiled to himself. Let the danger come! From now on, he would live dangerously!

When he entered the salon, he found that his sister was not alone. Sitting on a white sofa was a lady, whom Herr Faustini's sister introduced as her best friend, Luna. Frau Luna was wrapped in a dress with such large, luminous flowers that it was hard to tell where her contours began and where they ended. For example, the white sofa was so overrun with the giant flowers from her dress, that little of the sofa seemed to remain. Herr Faustini had to focus all of his energy in order to keep himself from spending the rest of the day staring at Frau Luna's flowery dress. When he felt her hand in his, images that tasted like cinnamon flitted through his mind. How many years had it been since he had eaten anything with cinnamon in it? Herr Faustini felt a strong pull that emanated from the fullness of her power and seemed to draw him toward the middle of her body. Frau Luna's gaze was warm, but it was a warmth that reminded Herr Faustini of the unimaginable sweetness of resin, in the midst of which certain plant species bind themselves until the end of their short lives. Frau Luna was still holding his hand, as he struggled against mental images whose provenance remained murky to him. He saw himself lying with this woman on a lounge, a piece of furniture which people long ago had called an ottoman. Golden arm bands tinkled on her wrist, like those seen in belly dance performances, and as she popped plump grapes into his mouth, he consumed them unquestioningly. He felt warm, very warm. In this vision, he was wearing harem pants that were strapped around his calves. He withdrew his hand awkwardly.

"Frau Luna is a talented painter," his sister commented. "This is only one of her many gifts. But you will see this for yourself. Oh, I'm so happy that you've met."

"Your sister has told me a lot about you, my dear," Frau Luna said. "I could hardly wait to meet you."

Herr Faustini nodded, as if he were in an empty gymnasium, and he heard himself respond: "The pleasure is all mine."

At this moment, it also occurred to him that the body shaping cream would be a much more suitable present for Frau Luna. His sister, on the other hand, had a slender waist as always, for which she had to thank her regular workouts at the local fitness club.

Herr Faustini's sister served coffee and cake. "You should know that my brother is a jewel, dear Luna. You just have to first get him out into the light. This first step is now accomplished. Isn't that true, dear brother?"

Herr Faustini's sister was a charming person. Herr Faustini thought this, too. When they were younger, the two of them had understood each other wonderfully. And when she had followed her husband abroad, Herr Faustini's world had become a poorer place. But now, in her house with its view of Lago Maggiore, in her salon by coffee and cake with the brightly draped Luna, his sister had become a stranger to him.

"Luna paints pictures inspired by music, isn't that true, Luna?"

"My pictures are music in color," explained Frau Luna. "I refuse to ever paint without music. Last week, I finished my *Lohengrin*. It was like a rush. What am I saying: it was a rush! Do you like Wagner, Herr Faustini?"

Herr Faustini had just placed a piece of cake in his mouth, so he smiled as obligingly as he could. And even as he swallowed, he tried to keep his smile from slipping.

"Of course, you like Wagner. You have to like Wagner once you have heard the true Wagner performed. And the only place to really hear the true Wagner played is Bayreuth. I go there every year. Do you know Bayreuth?"

Herr Faustini pursed his lips in preparation for his reply.

"Your sister has promised to come with me next time. It would be heavenly if all three of us could go together to hear the true Wagner performed!" Frau Luna maneuvered a piece of cake into her mouth.

"I'm looking forward to introducing you to my guests this evening," remarked Herr Faustini's sister. "They're all so anxious to meet you. I've told them everything about you, and they keep asking me when I'm going to introduce them to my brother. As time has passed, I have come close to losing my belief that I actually still have a brother."

-17-

The party was a success. Two gentlemen played saxophone and guitar, and four ladies, including Frau Luna, sang songs like "Yellow Submarine" and "When I'm Sixty-Four" for Herr Faustini's sister. Three of the four women had shortly trimmed, gray hair, and as they swayed back and forth in time to the music, Herr Faustini fleetingly saw moles in their places. He quickly shook his head and banished the image. There was prolonged applause after each of the songs.

As the ladies finished their concert in the midst of numerous hugs, Herr Faustini's sister stood there and wiped tears from her eyes. She thanked her friends from the bottom of her heart. Now she wanted to introduce to everyone her brother, who had made the trip and was visiting her for the first time since she had come to Ascona. She held her hand out toward Herr Faustini. Weak in the knees, he grasped his sister's outstretched hand and turned toward the guests. He smiled shyly into the circle, as he had seen people on television do when they accepted honorary awards.

After such a stressful experience, Herr Faustini went in search of a drink. On his way to the bar area, a glowing young woman approached him, and with sparkling eyes, she introduced herself as his niece Iris. He was overwhelmed. The way she placed her hand in his reminded him of the moment of happiness that she had once given him. Herr Faustini felt torn, because the calm and trusting hand he was holding rested there as if it had never been anywhere else. His eyes, however, beheld a beauty, a woman of the world, whose gaze considered him closely, searching for her uncle and the stranger that he had become to her. Herr Faustini grasped her hand longer than was typically acceptable, but her hand also seemed to feel comfortable in this location. He could feel deep in his chest how his reserves of strength were being mobilized and accelerated. He stood there as his face reddened, refusing to shift his gaze from his lovely niece, and he stammered something about how delighted he was to be here and how long it had been and how he knew she was living in Boston, where she was studying at Berklee College of Music. He could not really register what Iris said to him, although he listened very carefully to each word. It was difficult for him to link the words together and process them in their proper order — that was how amazed he was about who had developed from the girl who had once nestled her hand in his.

His sister had been so fortunate. She had to be the happiest person in the world to have such a daughter as Iris. And as he chatted with Iris, an abyss of loneliness opened up inside of him, a rift that must have been lurking there for all the years since he had last seen her. Everything was a failure. His life was one single delusion, as revealed by the hand of this wonderful person who was his niece. His life was defined by applied egoism. Otherwise, how could he live as if there were nothing and nobody in the world except himself? And his cat.

Life itself was everything; it was the highest and greatest good, and now he was holding the hand of life itself. And it was the greatest, and he was nothing and a worm. Years ago, he had played with the idea of adopting a child. He had even made inquiries about the formalities he would have to go through. They told him that an unmarried person was not permitted to adopt a child. He needed a partner, and both spouses had to be at least eighteen years older than the adopted child and to be living in acceptable circumstances. He had never even gotten as far as asking what was meant by "acceptable circumstances." Everything was a failure, if you did not cherish life, if you did not devote yourself to life, to a marvelous person, like his sister had done for her daughter Iris. He, the childless, was devoid of life. The chasm was ugly and dark, and it would never disappear.

WOLFGANG HERMANN

Averting his eyes, Herr Faustini excused himself from Iris and hurried away. She should not see him this way, her ever-absent uncle as a completely empty space. He went to his room and stared at a pillow he did not know.

Late that evening, Herr Faustini found a furtive moment to give his sister his birthday present. She studied the body shaping cream and said: "Sometimes you amaze me, dear brother." Then she hugged him.

After that, Herr Faustini slipped over to the buffet and claimed a glass of prosecco. When he turned back around, Frau Luna was standing in front of him. He noticed that under her colorful drapery, a capacious bosom swelled forward.

"Would you like to come by my atelier tomorrow? I'll be there all afternoon. I plan to work on my *Meistersinger*. It would mean a lot to me if you would come. After all, there is this strange familiarity that I have felt toward you since the moment we met…"

Herr Faustini took a big drink, looking a little abashed.

"Well then, tomorrow," she continued. "Would two o'clock work for you?"

Two o'clock worked as well for him as any other time. Herr Faustini nodded and fetched two glasses of prosecco. She thanked him with a little hot flash and downed half her glass in a single gulp.

-18-

Waking up in a strange bed was still something that Herr Faustini could not imagine. Now it was a fact. He was astonished at how well he had slept. And this had happened even though everything in this room was strange to him, from the scent of the bed sheets to the glistening light that filtered through the crack between the curtains. Herr Faustini wanted to get up and set out the food for the cat. But then he recalled that Frau Gigele was looking after the cat, so there was actually no reason to get up. Or was he feeling something like curiosity? For example, what did the view of the lake look like early in the morning? Herr Faustini left his bed, pushed apart the curtains, and was dazzled by the beauty. How could one bear up under so much loveliness? Not even five arm lengths away from him, an agave was blooming the single flower of its existence. The intense colors of the south were a rapture for his eyes. He told himself that he would have to take in this joy in small dosages. Could you ever grow accustomed to something like this? Would your senses eventually dull, and would you come to find all of this as normal, if you saw it every day?

After his morning toilette, he got dressed. The maid was just setting up breakfast out on the terrace as Herr Faustini emerged, blinking. He had not seen his sister's husband except for a short interchange with him at the party, which had been limited to not much more than a totally disinterested formal query on the part of his brother-in-law about how he was doing, and an equally short response and return query from Herr Faustini. A more direct altercation with Herr Head Physician and Cosmetic Surgeon could no longer be avoided, though. Herr Faustini was a guest in this house, the lord and master of which was his brother-in-law. Thus, it was only right and proper that they should engage in a conversation. The gaze alone which greeted him as he walked onto the terrace was enough to discourage him. This look contained a professional superiority honed over many years, which seemed totally unflappable, regardless of who was standing in front of him. This was coupled with an individualized and scalable hubris and disinterest, dependent on the other person in question, assuming that the other person was not a member of the golf club in which his brother-in-law played a prominent role, a dignitary from the Lions Club, or another notable of high degree. Reflected in his brother-in-law's eyes, Herr Faustini saw himself as a failure. He could dismiss his culpability in this perception due to the fact that in his brother-in-law's world, anyone like Herr Faustini was a failure, a person about whom it was best to hold your tongue. After a short greeting and an awkward moment of silence, the lord of the house exclaimed that he was so sorry but he needed to hurry to the clinic. He wished Herr Faustini a nice day, as he pulled out his cell phone and started dialing a number. With his characteristic tongue-clicking, he waited for the other person to pick up.

On the other hand, breakfast with the lady of the house was very pleasant. Brother and sister reminisced together about events from their childhoods, laughing loudly and often. As Herr Faustini told the story about how the neighboring farmer had once caught both of them consuming ears of corn in his cornfield, his sister grasped his shoulder as she shook with laughter. This warmed his heart, since it indicated that she had effortlessly crossed the boundaries that her social status had erected around her, and was still his dear sister.

The maid was serving flutes of Bellini mixed with peach puree, a delicacy that Herr Faustini had never tasted before today, as a suntanned Iris crossed the terrace. She had gone swimming in the lake, she explained. The water had been gloriously crystalline and refreshing. Herr Faustini almost sighed aloud at the contentment in her gaze. She once again stretched out her calm, warm hand with a naturalness that made him happy. Good God, he would have missed all this if he had not traveled here! He would have spent forever as a donkey, knowing nothing about the simple, deep power of a smile at the breakfast table. How easy the hours spent with dear ones could be, and how quickly they passed! As he watched Iris's bright eyes and listened to her stories about life in Boston, Herr Faustini wordlessly begged that this moment be allowed to last for ages. He realized that he needed to change his life. It was not too late for this, although he still needed to figure out the exact details.

-19-

The atelier was a spacious apartment, commanding a view of Lago Maggiore. Frau Luna led Herr Faustini through the separate rooms, their walls covered in large oil paintings. She called a deep red painting *Fire Face*, which she claimed to have painted in response to Schönberg's "Verklärte Nacht." Next to it hung a murky color labyrinth with the title *Brahms, Vier Ernste Gesänge*. She reverentially led Herr Faustini past a painting in which he recognized little else besides interconnecting color spirals.

"That is my latest *Lohengrin*," commented Frau Luna. "It is the first *Lohengrin* that I've really been happy with."

As she said this, she watched Herr Faustini through narrowed eyes. She lifted her arm as an orange veil floated across his eyes.

He retreated one step after the other. It was like

a train pulling out from a station: he was not sure if he was moving or if it was the room that was slowly closing in on him. It was so easy to sink backward. She was on top of him in an instant. She wafted musk and gazed at him with the eyes of a hunter. She opened his shirt, and as she reached each button, she sighed, "You."

Her tongue was everywhere. As she sucked on his ear, he almost burst out laughing. She deftly undid his pants with an invisible hand. Down there, she moved around at will, as if she had always been entitled to access. Her lips meandered between his legs, and she sucked on his manhood as if she had finally discovered the Fountain of Youth. While she did this, his gaze traced the color spirals in the last *Lohengrin*, although he kept losing himself in the muddled areas. He stumbled numbly through the thick undergrowth. Moss clung to his pant legs, his hands fumbled in the damp grass. There was no end in sight here, while at the same time, the beginning was just as elusive. At some point, she sank heavily and breathlessly down on top of him. Herr Faustini realized that the bed posts were made of sturdy, fine wood, not like the veneer he had at home.

-20-

As they sat on the terrace by the lake and savored ice cream sundaes, Herr Faustini's sister explained that Luna's deceased husband had held an important position at one of the large banks. "Unfortunately, they were unable to have any children. Luna's life has not been an easy one, but painting has been a great support for her. She has friends, yes indeed, very popular! She's attractive, don't you think?"

Herr Faustini nodded politely.

"She has so many talents! You absolutely must get to know her better! She has taste. She can read cards. Sometimes I really think that she can see the future. At least, everything she predicted about me has come true."

"What did she predict about you?" Herr Faustini wanted to know.

Herr Faustini's sister smiled knowingly, as she

moved on: "And she has money. At our age, we're allowed to talk about money, which has become an
overly negative topic lately. More than anyone else,
the young think that they can scorn money. A trifle, as
long as their parents are paying! No, there's no need to
feel ashamed if you respect money and value its bene-
ficial effects. I think it would be good for you to think
a little more about yourself," commented Herr Faustini's sister. "Your old jacket, for example, has seen better
days, if I may say so. Luna agrees," she added.

Herr Faustini cast an evaluative glance over his
jacket, as he stuck a spoonful of ice cream into his
mouth.

"A man such as yourself should think about
his old age," his sister remarked. "After all, you're
not getting any younger. And isn't Luna a fabulous
woman?"

She again studied him appraisingly. Herr Faustini strove to look as inconspicuous as possible. "She has
so many things going for her. I can't think of a single
negative about her. Can you think of any cons?" Herr
Faustini's sister asked.

Herr Faustini shook his head briefly and mat-
ter-of-factly.

"There you go," Herr Faustini's sister concluded
in relief. "Not a single negative. Where else could you
find such a woman? By her side, you'd get out more.
Bayreuth! Monte Carlo! Geneva! And every spring,

the San Remo Flower Parade. She's simply marvelous. A real sweetheart!"

Herr Faustini saw an excursion ship out on the lake. On the deck, he could make out a woman in a dark pink dress. She was turning her head into the wind, the way he had seen Frau Luna do. Suddenly he knew that it was time to leave. A person simply belonged where he belonged. This thought crossed his mind. Ask the cat why he lives where he lives. And ask Frau Gigele if she would fit better anywhere else. And ask the two flowerpots that Frau Gigele has hopefully been watering, what they think.

-21-

Herr Faustini's old jacket was worn out, according to his sister. The jacket that had served him so long and well. Not only long and well: Herr Faustini had become one with his jacket. At first, he had worn his jacket, because after all, that was what one did with jackets. However, only recently had he realized that his jacket protected him, provided him cover. He could conceal himself in his jacket, and nobody noticed. His jacket had been his home, his cave. His shell, his peacock feathers.

Herr Faustini was warm. He realized that he was sweating. He felt torn as he faced saying goodbye to his favorite piece of clothing, the one that was his home. Should he simply allow himself to part ways with his jacket without even the slightest resistance? Wasn't it time to be a man and stand up for his jacket's infinite superiority? Yet, hadn't Maria taught him that ev-

ery item in his possession was only there for a limited amount of time? Hadn't she taught him the most
important lesson of all: of how to say goodbye? And
where else could it be easier to say goodbye than here,
in this other light that so greatly softened the outlines
of things? Herr Faustini scrutinized his jacket, which
in this other light, actually did look a little shabby. Or
was it the environment, the strangers around him, that
had altered his perspective?

Herr Faustini's sister claimed that her daughter
Iris would be delighted to help her uncle go shopping.
Herr Faustini's face brightened. His sister still knew
him. Iris materialized with a smile on her face. "Are we
leaving?" she asked her uncle, who nodded gratefully.

Herr Faustini wandered through the pedestrian zone with Iris. They lingered in front of numerous
men's clothing shop windows. At one of them, a tweed
suit caught Herr Faustini's eye, and Iris nodded. As he
tried on this suit, Herr Faustini felt like a different person. The suit itself straightened his spine. He walked
proudly, stately through the shop, and gazed self-as-
suredly into the mirror. Could all of this really be contained in this suit? Did this suit possess the power to
turn Herr Faustini into another person? Iris nodded
and smiled her most winsome smile. Herr Faustini did
not take the suit back off again. Would he ever be able
to wear anything else again? The salesman packed up
his old jacket with the tips of his fingers. It was impos-

sible for him to bring the old jacket along with him into his new life, the one he would now lead thanks to the tweed suit. Herr Faustini left a handsome tip behind in the clothing shop, since after all, this traditional establishment was not a mass-market store. This new suit conveyed to him an unprecedented strength.

Herr Faustini asked Iris if he could treat her to an ice cream. Iris accepted the offer with a smile. The tweed suit absolutely needed to be celebrated.

"I should confess something to you," Herr Faustini said. "Without you, I never would have bought a new suit."

Iris ordered an extra-large mixed ice cream. Herr Faustini recalled earlier times and ordered a hot fudge sundae with the passionate enthusiasm of a butterfly hunter who had finally caught the last, missing exotic specimen for his collection. With a grin, Iris mimicked Herr Faustini's momentary hot-fudge-sundae excitement. As Herr Faustini watched her, he realized that it had been a long time since he had felt as happy as he did at this moment. He felt like a vessel through which flowed nothing except gratitude and tenderness. He went to the restroom because he did not want Iris to see his emotional state. In the restroom mirror, Herr Faustini still looked like a new person. He greeted this new person with a jaunty little wave.

Iris had to go to her yoga class. Herr Faustini escorted her to the door of the class location. She kissed him goodbye on the cheek and hurried on. Herr Faustini bought an ochre-colored rose and made his way to Frau Luna's studio. Luna opened the door and wrapped her arms around his neck. Herr Faustini conjured forth the rose, earning himself another kiss. Luna was ecstatic to see him. Before he could even say a word, he found himself sitting at Luna's table with a cup of coffee in hand. Over and over, Luna praised his handsome new suit. Only first in this suit was it clear who Herr Faustini truly was. A thoroughly elegant gentleman! She had seen from the start that this elegance was hidden inside him. The tweed suit really showed it off nicely. She congratulated him on his taste. Herr Faustini thanked her for her compliment, his voice rather small and pained. Frau Luna asked if he was feeling alright. Certainly, Herr Faustini assured her, everything was just fine. He simply needed to say goodbye. He had to get back, since there were things that required his attention back home. They were probably already worried about him.

"Who would be worried?" Frau Luna asked testily. She thought there was only the cat there.

Herr Faustini's mouth twitched upward, not willing to obey him as usual. A smile came close to escaping. "Only it was really lovely here," he replied. And he would like to come back. At some point.

Clouds now skimmed across Frau Luna's eyes, which had been radiantly cheerful only a moment before. She went into the kitchen, while Herr Faustini stood up. She returned with a handkerchief, and he held his hand out to her. She embraced him, pulling him tightly against her. After he reached the door, he turned back around, and he saw a tear cut a wide streak through her makeup.

-22-

"**D**o you really have to leave already?" his sister wondered at the bus station.

"Please stay longer, Uncle," Iris urged with her prettiest pout.

Herr Faustini hugged both of them. If he did not leave now, he would be incapable of ever getting away. He would return soon, he promised. Through the bus window, the square he was now leaving reminded him of a darkened movie theater, where all the other viewers around him were making ample use of their handkerchiefs. As usual, he did not have one on him.

-23-

Summer was ending. The autumnal light was once again calling forth the great glowing from the insides of things. Soon the fall fog would slowly extinguish this luster. Herr Faustini missed the days of transitioning, since these had fallen within the time he had been gone. Although his trip had been brief, he was still confused. It was not easy for him to get his feet back on the ground, which had almost become a little strange to him. Even the cat seemed to hardly recognize him. In the evening, he did not come to him to be petted.

Frau Gigele had fed him, watered the flowering plants, set the mail on the kitchen table. She had put things in order, at least that was the way it seemed to Herr Faustini. His house had never before seemed so empty. It looked unoccupied and absent. No human warmth clung to the curtains, no laughter lingered in

the corner. The armchair resembled a relic from another time. Not a soul had sat in it for at least a century.
Though it was still summer, all of the rooms seemed
cool, as if winter had sent its chill early, in order to
conceal it in Herr Faustini's house. He would not have
been shocked if icicles had grown underneath his armchair.

The next morning the cat meowed around the
house, as if it were starving. Herr Faustini set out his
dish with a smile. The cat squinted up at him and
brushed around his legs. The link was reestablished.

The ground on which Herr Faustini walked was
once again the ground he was used to. However, Herr
Faustini was now sensitive to the ground's hardness,
to the way the sky pressed darkly down onto it, unlike
in Ascona, where the air expanded into ever widen-
ing spaces. And he noticed that his world was small
— much more than small, it was tight and barren. He
proceeded home, where the meadow was suffused in
its own ring of light. Or was that simply a transforma-
tion caused by the house's old window glass?

Herr Faustini sat for a few moments in front of
his house, in order to provide the new neighbor an opportunity to visit. But he remained invisible, and stayed
that way over the coming days. Had perhaps all of the
dangling shutters been straightened once and for all?
Had he moved on to somewhere he was still needed?

With each morning, the fog clung longer and

longer to the meadows. The autumnal silence had settled around the house. A thick carpet of withering leaves was spread underneath the apple tree. The cat now rubbed against Herr Faustini's legs as usual. These days Herr Faustini typically left the house early. He felt a need to make good use of the days. Soon the endless fall rains would arrive, and the snow would also not hold off long. He sensed a hunger for his landscape, a longing to absorb the images of it before it faded into the cold fog. He wanted to experience the stillness of empty time, before it vanished into a hole in the earth. He had not seen stray time in quite a while. He knew he had to seek it out.

-24-

Once again, a Sunday lay resolutely around the area. What could be done to purge from the world this bulky, doughy mass that brought all movement to a standstill? Herr Faustini sensed the glimmering of a broader horizon from beyond the mountains. Yet the Sunday was unavoidable, and the numbness it gave off did not respect national borders. All of a sudden, strange pictures swirled before his eyes. Street sellers in narrow lanes, peddling tethered chickens, the soft parts of unknown animals floating in vinegar water. There were no Sundays in this teeming bustle of eyes, voices, and dogs skittering and scurrying between legs. Astonished, he wandered through the lanes of this completely unknown land. He had never seen so much poverty as among these people, who were carrying their earthly belongings on their backs, as they grasped the hands of children who peered with wide eyes into the world's mystery. To Herr Faustini's imaginary ear, these people's language sounded like lute music, as it trickled down to him like a fine rivulet. He stroked his cheek absentmindedly and noticed that the moist air of this distant land lay softly across his skin. His eyes were wide open in this other light, and on the glistening horizon, he could make out the fine tracery of the branches of a strange tree. Regardless of how foreign this distant land and its people were, Herr Faustini was amazed at how similar most of this was to his own little world. The unknown was embodied in a different, thicker light, other scents and voices like a quiet carillon.

In the midst of the tangle of people, a man in a perfectly pressed, double-breasted suit appeared before his mind's eye. He twirled an ivory cane in his hand, his shoes shining spotlessly. He wandered through the market lane with a gaze that was not focused either far away or close at hand. This man was an island, as he strode forward with a motionless face. It was the black prince. In the midst of the garishly clothed summer tourists, he strolled along in his double-breasted suit, swinging the ivory cane. He carried a space around him, his own calm. Timid gazes trailed him, but no one spoke to him. For years, the black prince had walked like this along the lake, with the same gaze into nowhere. However, now the black prince was moving through the light of the unknown, yet he was just as serene and disconnected from the rest of the world as he had been in the lake park where Herr Faustini had spoken to him and asked him how he was doing. In the distant red-gold light, in which Herr Faustini now saw the black prince walking, he took a risk once more and greeted him warmly.

"Hello, Your Highness, I see that you have not changed. I hope that you are doing well?"

The prince nodded amicably. "I'm doing very well," he said.

"It is marvelous here among these people. Is it true, Your Highness, that you are a prince from the Ivory Coast?" Herr Faustini inquired.

"My family lives in Abidjan," the prince replied. "Yes, I come from a chief's family. I have not seen my family in a long time. It has been almost ten years. I have spent most of this time in Bregenz, Pension Weidach. Bregenz is a nice city. If only the winters weren't so long. I can't seem to get used to the winters, unfortunately. While I freeze, the bananas are growing at home. I had my first coat made in Vienna, but the cold works its way through my coat. That's why I don't spend much time outside during the winter. What I miss the most is the view of the sea. For me, the sea means freedom, even if I'm not a sailor and I only know the sea from the land. Bregenz is the only place, far and wide, where I can see the distance. The view of the lake helps me breathe. But the lake is not the sea. I can look out across the lake as long as I like, but it will never turn into the sea. I have spent many months staring at the ceiling in my room at Pension Weidach. It is amazing what all can cross your mind. The only thing you must not lose is your strength. If I lose my strength, my skin will become thin like a banana that is not growing well. When that happens, I talk to our village elder. I tell him about my life in Bregenz and complain about my sorrow. He listens, even though he has been dead for many years. He listens to me and sends me strength. I can feel the strength returning to me. I can still see them, all my people in Abidjan, where I can never return. But I am connected with them. I'm the only one from my family who is living abroad. I am like a fruit that has fallen far from its tree."

"What can I do to help you get back to your tree?" Herr Faustini asked the black prince in his imagination.

"I am with my family, even when I'm standing and freezing in a drafty bus station in Bregenz. The Earth is a large house with many rooms, but all of the rooms come together to build the same house. That's why there is no loneliness for those who know that they are in constant contact with anyone and everyone. That's why it doesn't matter if I'm lying in my room in Bregenz in Pension Weidach and staring at the ceiling. In reality, I'm with my family in Abidjan. Don't your wise men say that the world turns? I can't feel this happen, but I can think about it. And when it turns, it means that each location on the planet is equally far away. With every passing moment, the Earth returns to itself. Thus, the expanding of the world is an illusion. There is no distance. Each location on Earth is situated at the same distance. Pension Weidach is a good place to consider such things. I'm in the midst of my family, even if some of them are already dead. I'm with them. I can see a web of bright threads before me, and I am in this net, as well as my family. The connections never dissolve; do you understand? It is impossible for the connections to dissolve. Bregenz is Abidjan. Abidjan is Bregenz. Can you see the web too?"

Herr Faustini saw the web. It was not a web like he knew from spiders. It was a web of glowing threads of pure light. Each thread led to a person, whom he saw glowing in their own light. The people he saw were no longer separate, and he did not only see them. They were around him, in him.

He decided to search out the black prince and offer to drive him to the sea. He wanted to see the sea reflected in the eyes of the prince. And he wanted to see it for himself, because he had never been to the sea. It could not continue like this.

Herr Faustini walked hurriedly out to the suburban Pension Weidach. He asked, "Is there an elegant black gentleman living here?"

"Who is supposed to be staying here?" the landlady asked resentfully.

"I'm looking for the gentleman from the Ivory Coast, who is living here."

"Oh, him," responded the landlady. She studied Herr Faustini closely. It appeared that nobody had asked about the black prince over all the long years.

"Should I call him?"

"That's unnecessary," Herr Faustini claimed.

"Room One," said the landlady, "on the second floor."

Herr Faustini walked up the stairwell through a wall of cold cigarette smoke. The landlady almost dislocated her neck as she strained to watch him, until he reached the next floor. Herr Faustini realized that his heart had jumped into his throat. Here he was, standing at the door for Room 1 as the personification of harassment. The prince certainly would place no value on his visit. What if he simply turned him away? Herr Faustini cautiously knocked on the door. Silence. He waited a few moments before knocking even harder. Something moved inside. The key turned in the door. The black prince stood wearily in the doorframe. His eyes were as murky as a river at flood stage.

"Qu'est-ce que vous voulez?" the prince inquired.

"My name is Faustini," said Herr Faustini. "I would like to talk to you."

Herr Faustini saw nothing in these eyes to indicate that his revelation had been welcomed.

"I apologize for the interruption, but I wanted to speak with you. I have a proposal for you."

"*Comment?*" the prince asked. "A proposal?"

"You told me that every place in the world is situated at the same distance as every other one. The expansion of the Earth is an illusion, because with each passing moment, each location on the planet is equally far away. That's what you said. Bregenz is Abidjan, Your Highness."

"Abidjan," the prince murmured. "*Abidjan, c'est loin. Comment vous savez?*"

"The sea," Herr Faustini forged ahead. "The sea is out there, isn't it? And you have seen it! You come from the sea, Your Highness!"

"The sea," the prince said, "is infinitely far from here."

"But there is no distance, right? Then let's go on a trip! We can get away from here and travel to the sea, Your Highness! That is what I wanted to propose to you. Travel with me to the sea!"

"The sea," the prince uttered quietly. "The sea no longer exists."

His golden eyes absorbed the last small beam of light, which had somehow gotten lost here in the dark hallway. The prince shut the door slowly.

"Listen," Herr Faustini called. "You told me that you are in constant contact with your ancestors. Ask them! Ask them if the sea no longer exists!"

The door opened again a crack.

"How do you know *toutes ces choses-là*?"

"You told me yourself!"

"I certainly did not, *nix, certainement je ne disais rien!*"

The prince closed the door and turned the key in the lock.

Herr Faustini stood there, powerlessly.

"Your Highness, I beg you to ask your village elder if the sea still exists! Please, Your Highness!"

Herr Faustini no longer recognized his own voice. Had it been the dismal corridor that had stolen the last ray of light from these surroundings? When had been the last time that he had felt so tired? He sat down on the floor with his back against the wall. His eyes lacked the strength to reach the gray wallpaper on the other side of the hall. How quickly strength could seep away. He ran his hand across the well-worn area rug he was sitting on. Had it swallowed up his strength? The rug sat there, devoid of secrets. There was nothing on this rug that could captivate a gaze. Herr Faustini's eyes were tired. He heard a distant rushing that grew increasingly clear, and he saw the sea before him, as it crashed toward the shore. As the wave receded, it was followed by the noise of a thousand pebbles cascading all at once, but already the next wave was approaching. The fullness, the emptiness, the fullness. The emptiness was only the flip side of the fullness, which was nothing without the emptiness. The sea was a muscle that expanded and contracted. The great sea — it still existed!

The key turned, and the door opened. The prince's golden eyes glowed.

"We will travel to the sea?" the prince asked. "To the real sea?"

Standing up, Herr Faustini replied: "Yes, dear prince. We will travel to the real sea."

"Tomorrow?" the prince inquired.

"Not tomorrow," Herr Faustini responded. "But the day after tomorrow."

-25-

The train flew across the land for many hours. Herr Faustini observed the world which spread out before him in its infinite newness. "Each location on the planet is equally far away," he whispered to himself. This was why every trip was possible.

"Every trip is possible," Herr Faustini commented.

"Every trip is possible," the prince repeated, his eyes gleaming above his violet double-breasted suit.

Herr Faustini just sat there in his new tweed suit and let himself be seen.

On the horizon, a group of people materialized. The air shimmered like the heat across a rural road. Their contours grew hazy, and they bodies seemed to blend, one with the other. At the front strode a person with a dark pink bundle on his shoulders. It was the parachute jumper. The man at his side was pushing a bicycle, and on his head, he was wearing a bike helmet.

Both of them were sunk in conversation. Frau Helga followed the two of them, as she chatted with Frau Gigele. Frau Nussbaumer walked behind both of them, and she nodded as the woman to whom Herr Faustini had given two euros on the lake promenade carried on about something, with sweeping, circular gestures. The two of them were followed at a leisurely pace by the man in the military jacket, who was focused on a dialogue with Herr Faustini's cleaning woman. Herr Ospelt was taking his dachshund for a walk. The man in the black turtleneck was engrossed in a discussion with the American artist. Iris walked arm in arm with Herr Faustini's sister, whereby the warmth of the younger woman's eyes formed a circle of light around her. Clad in the dress with the oversized flowers, Frau Luna followed them, her shoulders pulled back stiffly. At her heels, the swimmer in the short trousers strolled with a masculine step. Nicole from Salon Heaven had an ethereally beautiful smile on her lips. Her arm was linked in Frau Judith Robatscher's. The woman from the art center who had smiled so pleasantly at him waved at a stranger she could clearly see off in the distance. She was followed by the Polish dog breeder with Robin Hood tucked under his arm. The puppy snuffled the sleeve of the new neighbor, the self-described specialist in the straightening of dangling shutters. The tour bus from Swabia trailed this group, and the father and son with the sunglasses could be seen telling the bus driver the story about the missing crate in Frau Isele's house. The image of the cat purred, as it wound its way around Herr Faustini's legs.